P9-BYG-037

PRAISE FOR DOMENICO STARNONE'S *TIES*

DISCARDED

"*Ties* is about the unspoken mysteries that bind us, that push us away from each other and bring us back . . . [it is Starnone's] leanest, most understated and emotionally powerful novel."
—Rachel Donadio, *The New York Times Book Review*

"*Ties*, translated by Jhumpa Lahiri, seizes you and doesn't let go for 150 pages. The tone is cool and contained. Hysteria threatens, and is kept away—although only just."
—Laura Freeman, *The Times*

"Scalding and incisive."—*Library Journal* (Starred Review)

"The story glints and cuts like smashed crystal."—Anthony Cummins, *The Guardian*

"Absolutely gripping from start to finish."—Victoria Hislop, author of *The Island*

"*Ties* is brief, brilliant and unnerving."—Margot Livesey, author of *Mercury* and *The Flight of Gemma Hardy*

"A tight tale of domestic carnage."—Frances Wilson, *The Times Literary Supplement*

"Charmingly intimate, disarmingly chatty and laced with some walloping surprises, *Ties* is an expertly crafted short novel."—*Shelf Awareness*

"[*Ties* is] a slim, stunning meditation on marriage, fidelity, honesty, and truth."—*Kirkus Reviews* (Starred Review)

MAR 0 5 2018

DISCARDED

ALSO BY

DOMENICO STARNONE

First Execution
Ties

TRICK

Domenico Starnone

TRICK

*Translated from the Italian
by Jhumpa Lahiri*

Ventress Library
Marshfield, MA 02050

MAR 0 5 2018

Europa
editions

Europa Editions
214 West 29th Street
New York, N.Y. 10001
www.europaeditions.com
info@europaeditions.com

This book is a work of fiction. Any references to historical events,
real people, or real locales are used fictitiously.

Copyright © 2016 by Giulio Einaudi editore s.p.a., Torino
First Publication 2018 by Europa Editions

Translation by Jhumpa Lahiri
Original title: *Scherzetto*
Translation copyright © 2018 by Europa Editions

All rights reserved, including the right of reproduction
in whole or in part in any form.

Library of Congress Cataloging in Publication Data is available
ISBN 978-1-60945-444-9

Starnone, Domenico
Trick

Book design by Emanuele Ragnisco
www.mekkanografici.com

Inside illustrations by Dario Maglionico
Cover illustration, Dario Maglionico, detail from *Reificazione #9*, 2014.
Private collection

Prepress by Grafica Punto Print – Rome

Printed in the USA

CONTENTS

TRICK

INTRODUCTION
by Jhumpa Lahiri

Dolcetto o Scherzetto is Italian for "trick or treat," only inverted: the literal translation is *treat or trick*. A prankster's slogan that masked children, seeking something sweet, say in the dark, in a darkening season, on the thresholds of strangers' homes. The phrase, coined in America, is both solicitous and imperative, mirthful and menacing. When a child says, "trick or treat" on Halloween night, it's up to the adult either to play along or suffer the consequences.

And so I landed on *Trick* as an English title for *Scherzetto*, Domenico Starnone's fourteenth novel, even though until recently Halloween has had little traction in Italy, and nothing to do with this book. But when I translated the word *scherzetto* in one of the novel's key scenes, *trick* fell short. My spontaneous solution was the expression *gotcha,* and after completing the first draft, I asked Starnone if the Italian equivalent (*ti ho beccato*) conveyed the sense of *scherzetto.* Not really, he replied, adding that it was closer to a proposal: "Let's play around, let's have a little fun."

The adjective *little* is key; *scherzetto* is the diminutive of the noun *scherzo,* derived from the verb *scherzare,* which means, principally, to joke or to play. *Scherzi,* one quips in Italian to say, *you're kidding*. Musicians know that s*cherzo* indicates a vigorous movement in a composition, to be executed playfully. Note the associative, connective tissue rapidly forming between these words: trick, joke, kid, kidding, play.

Trick is an extremely playful literary composition. It's about a kid, dealing with a kid, having kids, kidding around. It's about how it feels when the joke's on you. In some sense, the real protagonist of this novel is not a person but a playing card: the Joker. A trump card, a wild card, a jester, a clown. A card of American origin whose identity is mutable, that can substitute for others. One might think that the word for Joker in Italian would have something to do with *scherzo*. Instead it's called a *Jolly*, an English adjective that has become an Italian noun, the imported etymology based on the fact that early versions of the card were called *the Jolly Joker*.

Borrowing, copying, converting, replacing, bleeding together: *Trick* is an ongoing act of juxtaposition, a thrust and parry in which two very different works of fiction confront, confound, and cross-pollinate one another. *Trick*, set in Naples, is about an aging illustrator commissioned to create images for a deluxe Italian edition of "The Jolly Corner," a celebrated ghost story by Henry James, published in 1908 and set in New York City. James was an American author who spent most of his life in Europe. Starnone is an Italian author, arguably the finest alive in that country today, who has spent considerable time reading Henry James.

The central action of *Trick*, spanning just four days, takes place in November, the darkest of months, and is steeped in gothic references: apparitions, howling winds, figures that disappear down corridors. It is about things that go bump in the night, people who ring doorbells and are not terribly kind. It is about the fear of slipping and falling, of failure, of illness, of facing phantoms, of facing death. Perhaps, in some sense, Halloween *does* have something to do with it: Like a flickering jack-o'-lantern, at once illuminating and terrifying, the whole novel can be read as a dialectic between darkness and light.

Trick makes us grin and at times makes us cackle with laughter, but it also unnerves, settling over us like a damp chill. Much of the discomfort derives from the narrator's ambivalent attitude toward Mario, his four-year-old grandson. Their relationship is always vacillating between affection and antagonism, solidarity and spite. Unlike his grandfather, a convalescent in his seventies tormented by his lack of vitality, Mario represents agility, potential, life in spades. Evolution is an underlying theme of this novel, and thus, survival of the fittest. One can read *Trick* as a domesticated version of *Lord of the Flies*, the island swapped for an apartment in Naples, the repercussions every bit as savage. Grandfather and grandson are marooned together, also pitted apart; both are essentially abandoned by the adult world.

The drama unfolds from the grandfather's point of view. He has a name, Daniele, but it is so seldom mentioned that one tends to overlook it. Mario, on the other hand, commands the spotlight. The child is at once precocious and innocent, unbearable and vulnerable. He can neither read nor tell time and yet he repeatedly outwits a man seven decades his senior. Daniele is protective, an anxious caregiver, but also palpably aggressive, neglectful, and mean. Mario's impulse to mimic his grandfather is poignant, and might be read as a form of flattery, but it is interpreted, by a puerile old man who bristles even at the term "nonno" ("grandfather" in Italian), as defeat. An epigraph for *Trick* might have come from Heraclitus: "Lifetime is a child at play, moving pieces in a game. Kingship belongs to the child" (fragment 123).

Like Mario and his grandfather, the very narrative weave of this novel is at loggerheads. It shuttles between witty dialogue and rich meditative passages, fast-paced action and scalding interior reflection. It is tonally bifurcated, serious and silly, lugubrious and lighthearted, ironic, desperate, full of bile. The Italian writer Goffredo Fofi points out that it is written in "two different registers." Conversations between characters are what push the story forward. But stepping back, the reader discovers a potent metafictional exchange between *Trick* and

"The Jolly Corner," as well as a series of broader analogies between New York and Naples, James and Starnone, language and image, present and past.

This novel reminds us that much of art is about communicating with the dead. There is no disputing the fact that *Trick* resembles—one might go so far as to say channels—"The Jolly Corner." Not surprisingly, both works are preoccupied by notions of similitude, simulacra, doubles, interchangeability. At first glance, the surprising kinship, independently forged by Starnone, seems straightforward: Both stories, simply put, are about the horror of returning to one's place of origin. But a close reading of these texts—and I highly recommend this— yields innumerable, more subtle points of contact—echoes, clues, inside jokes. True, the text of James's story hasn't been inserted between the covers of *Trick*, and Starnone's novel can be fully appreciated without reading a word of James. It would be a pity, though.

In addition to riffing consummately on "The Jolly Corner," *Trick* resuscitates James's work and themes more generally. I could not help but think of *Washington Square* (both works depict a charged father-daughter relationship and a problematic son-in-law figure); "The Turn of the Screw" (his most famous ghost story, about a frazzled adult left alone with a precocious child); "The Real Thing" (narrated by an illustrator, and all about the dichotomy between reality and representation); and "The Figure in the Carpet" (about a widowed husband, and a wife's secrets).

The convergence with James reaches its apogee, however, in the appendix to *Trick*, a sort of free-associating, illustrated artist's diary, tonally divergent, which glosses the main story and also constitutes its distilled essence. The appendix reverses gear, the entries spanning the weeks leading up to the novel's action. Drawings crowd the margins, both enhancing and crowding out the words. The appendix is an organ literally cut out of the story, seemingly extraneous but in fact fundamental to our understanding: an intimate commentary and also a tour-de-force in which sentences from James's story, in Italian translation, have been ingeniously spliced into the text. So, while Starnone and James remain separate authors of separate works of fiction, the appendix, itself a hybrid piece of writing, literally fuses them together. *Trick* is no mere homage to James; it is a willful act of combining, of appropriation, of grafting on both a thematic and linguistic plane.

Italy's love affair with American literature begins more or less around the time of Starnone's birth, in 1943, which coincides with the fall of Fascism. James was among the thirty-three largely unknown American authors translated for the first time in *Americana*, an anthology edited by Elio Vittorini, published in 1941, that profoundly influenced postwar Italian writing. Vittorini extolled Hemingway, Cesare Pavese famously translated *Moby Dick*. These writers did more than love American literature; they identified with it, drew hope and vitality from it. What Starnone does in *Trick*, more than seven decades after *Americana*, takes this love affair to new extremes, and renders an Italian writer's identification with an American novelist quite literal.

James is the obvious frame of reference, but there is another literary key I feel compelled to mention: Kafka. For *Trick* explores themes and preoccupations central to Kafka's vision. One, surely, is an obsession with the body: with physical discomfort, with weakness, with disease. The tragicomic description of an old man struggling to get out of bed in the morning on the first page of *Trick* reminded me of Gregor Samsa's immediate predicament following his metamorphosis. Mario's boundless physical prowess—he is always jumping, moving around, doing things—only exacerbates Daniele's sense of feeling debilitated, constrained. Much of their friction can be summed up as a contrast between bodies: one small and mighty, the other large, laid low.

Kafka, like the narrator of *Trick*, had an aversion toward children. Elias Canetti observes, "Thus it is really envy that Kafka feels in the presence of children . . . an envy coupled with disapproval." *Trick* is very much about envy: generational, professional, sexual. Like the narrator of *Trick*, Kafka also detested his father. The compressed, recondite appendix recalls the sensibility of Kafka's own *Diaries*, a heterodox merging of observation and storytelling. And, finally: *Trick* shares, with Kafka, and with James for that matter, a charged relationship to physical space, and the frequent need for open air. Most of *Trick*'s action is set indoors, or on thresholds. The tension between inside and outside is ongoing, similar to the play between darkness and light. But the most memorable scene of the novel takes place on a balcony: a platform perched over nothing, a space that plays with space itself.

The balcony, in *Trick*, is a locus of risk and of refuge, of exile as well as freedom. It is rejection of family and origins, and also reeks of those very origins. It is a place where one is permitted to see beyond, to project. The balcony represents the precarious state of everything: youth, fame, relationships, life itself. Anything can break off, plummet at a moment's notice. This existential anxiety is the mass of air upon which the novel paradoxically rests. The void represents emptiness, death, but also creation. For this is the artist's habitat: turned away from a secure foundation, creating from nothing.

There are extraordinary passages in this novel about what it means to become an artist, about the mechanics and mystery of inspiration. It describes what happens when an artist begins to slow down, struggle, question his own production. Making art is a form of playing, a game the artist plays for tremendous stakes. Starnone plays with James; perhaps he is also playing with Kafka, an author, along with Calvino, whom he often cites as a literary forefather. Calvino played vigorously with his reader, his characters, with genre, the essence of narrative itself, as did Pirandello, Svevo, and Nabokov. Starnone is a player on this team.

An attentive reader of Starnone will find further interplay among his previous works. Certainly *Spavento* (a novel largely about illness, whose title means *fear* in Italian), *Via Gemito* (about childhood in Naples, about a hateful and hated father), and *Ties* (about defining ourselves, growing older, and what binds one generation to the next). *Trick* stems from this body of work but is its own creature, inventive at its very core. Of course, this is all speculation on my part. Starnone is a writer who knows never to show his full hand.

The underlying theme, visited again and again in Starnone, is identity: Who are we, where and what do we come from, why do we become what we become? In *Trick*, more succinctly than ever, he examines heredity, the effects of coupling, what is handed down, what slips through the cracks. Identity, for Starnone, is never singular but multiple, never static, always in flux. Identity entails selection, assortment, happenstance, strategy, risk. This is why the principal metaphor in *Trick* is a deck of cards, which spawns the act of *discarding*: shunning possibilities, setting them aside, whittling down options in order to shape ourselves, our futures. Not surprisingly, the novel pays special attention to adolescence, a phase in which a child's body is violently reacting, expanding, and altering itself, a phase at the end of which we are expected to choose our path and become an adult. The novel confronts the tension between what lies in the cards and the consequence of playing the cards we're dealt. What ultimately haunts is the hypothetical (a conditional construction particularly dear to Italian grammar, and consciousness): what one might have been, how things might have turned out. Like Spencer Brydon in "The Jolly Corner," the protagonist of *Trick* is assaulted less by who he's become than by what he didn't, by what James calls "all the old baffled foresworn possibilities."

The word *scherzetto* also means "a minor work or composition" in Italian. But there is nothing minor about this novel apart from Mario, who is indeed quite small. *Trick* is not a story for children, nor is it a novel for those in need of reassurance. Here is the fine print that most of us prefer to ignore as we blunder through life. It warns us that childhood is scary, as is falling in love and getting married, as is old age. We are prey to rage along the way: at one's parents, one's offspring, one's choices, one's own blood. And there is no escape from fear: of who we really are, of what we see and what we don't.

I translated *Trick* more or less one year exactly after translating *Ties*, Starnone's previous novel. In some sense, I had a running start, given that I was already familiar with the author's pacing, tics, fixations. But *Trick* was trickier. The title remains a compromise, only a partial solution. This novel also contains Neapolitan dialect, new territory for me. The use of dialect underscores the tonal double register, and also represents the protagonist's hostile relationship to himself, his city of origin, his past. Some of this dialect I intuited. Other terms, rife with violence and obscenity, were politely translated for me into Italian by Starnone himself.

Certain wordplay was impossible to capture. What to do, for example, with a term like *schizzar via*? It appears in a passage which describes the balcony, and is used to convey the tenuous connection between a building and the cantilevered platform that protrudes. I translated it as "flying off." But *schizzare* refers to liquids, too. It's the water flicked between Mario and his grandfather when they say "scherzetto" to each other (though in that scene, Starnone opts for a close cousin, *spruzzare*). *Schizzare* refers to fluids that burst, that hemorrhage. In the opening paragraph, we learn that the artist-protagonist of *Scherzetto* has undergone surgery followed by blood loss, a transfusion. Serendipitously, *schizzo* is also the word for a drawing, a sketch, the first draft of a book.

Trezziare was another dilemma, another delight. It's a strictly Neapolitan verb that refers to the card game *tresette*, and refers to the slow reveal of cards in hopes of finding the "three" that wins the game. But it has a broader meaning in Neapolitan culture, used to describe the sensation of joyfully anticipating something, for example, the way a child counts down to Christmas. It's a word tailor-made for *Trick*, a term that stitches together many of its myriad themes. In Italian, one slowly savors the full range of meaning, of reverberations. In English, much of this linguistic complexity drains away.

To translate is to walk down numerous scary corridors, to grope in the dark. I took my cue from the illustrator-protagonist of *Trick*. In the appendix he writes, "thoroughly knowing the text is the first step to working properly." This was what I did, reading and rereading not just Starnone but James, first in English, then in Italian translation, thereby both closing the circle and forming a triangle. Translation, much like this novel, is the intersection of two texts and voices, but a legitimate translation of *Trick* required three players: Starnone, James, and me.

Reading "The Jolly Corner" in English after translating *Trick* was something like walking through a hall of mirrors. Sentences, words, images, and motifs began to emerge, to startle me, recognizable but distorted. *Trick* rewards the reader who looks carefully. Like "The Jolly Corner," it plays with optics, with the eye and with "I." To read both texts is to experience an act of ongoing mutual illumination, each text serving as an annotation and alter ego of the other.

The more I moved between texts the more I marveled. Starnone uses languages the way a great painter works with color, conjuring the illusion of three dimensions from a blank flat surface. I spent days deepening my understanding of key terms in *Trick*: *scherzare, giocare, buio, rabbia, vuoto* (*joking, playing, darkness, rage, emptiness*). When Starnone plays with these words, he knows how to tease out and release their potential, how to shuffle their complex ontological identities, in brief how to *trezziare* with unparalleled finesse.

Scholars and critics will be playing for years with this novel, teasing out its various layers, links, correspondences. As a translator, I, too, had my share of fun. My version of *Trick*, the first in English, is just one of many that might have been. A translation is nothing if not a process of elimination. For every sentence I constructed, I had to discard numerous possibilities. A translation is also, by definition, the offshoot of a pre-existing text. My hope, immodest as it will sound, was to channel Starnone's style, to write as if he were writing, to somehow copy and paste him into English. This, too, involves something of a trick. A translation surgically alters the text's identity, insisting upon a foreign linguistic DNA, requiring a transfusion of alternate grammar and syntax. The generational bond between texts is indisputable. One descends from the other, and thus they remain connected, as distinct as they may be. Translation is an act of doubling and converting, and the resulting transformation is precarious, debatable even in its final form. Starnone's text remains the parent that spawned this translation, but somewhere along the road to its English incarnation, it also became a ghost.

TRICK

CHAPTER ONE

1.

One evening Betta called, crankier than usual, wanting to know if I felt up to minding her son while she and her husband took part in a mathematics conference in Cagliari. I'd been living in Milan for a couple of decades, and the thought of decamping to Naples, to the old house I'd inherited from my parents, and where my daughter had been living since prior to getting married, didn't thrill me. I was over seventy and, having been a widower for some time, had lost the habit of living with others. I only felt comfortable in my own bed and in my own bathroom. Furthermore, I'd undergone, a few weeks earlier, a small surgical procedure which, even in the clinic, seemed to have done more harm than good. Though the doctors poked their faces day and night into my room, to tell me that everything had gone fine, my hemoglobin was low, my ferritin was poor, and one afternoon, I saw small heads, plaster-white, stretching toward me from the opposite wall. They gave me a transfusion right away, the hemoglobin went up a little, and finally they sent me home. But now I was struggling to recover. In the mornings I was so feeble that in order to stand up I had to muster my strength, grasping my thighs with my fingers, bending my torso forward as if it were the top of suitcase, and stretching the muscles of my upper and lower limbs with a determination that took my breath away. And it was only when the back pain ebbed that I managed to lift my skeleton completely, cautiously however, detaching my fingers gently from my thighs and abandoning my arms at my sides with a wheezing that lingered until, finally, I reached an upright position. Which was why, to Betta's request, I automatically replied:

—Does this conference really mean a lot to you?

—It's work, Dad. I have to deliver the keynote and Saverio presents his paper the afternoon of the second day.

—How long will you be away?

—November twentieth to the twenty-third.

—So I'd have to stay with the child, alone, for four days?

—Sally comes every morning, she'll clean up and cook for you. And anyway, Mario is totally independent.

—No three-year-old is independent.

—Mario's four.

—Neither is a four-year-old. But that's not the point: I have urgent work to finish and I haven't even started.

—What do you have to do?

—Illustrate a story by Henry James.

—What's the story?

—A guy goes back to one of his former homes in New York and finds a ghost. That is, he finds who he would have been were he to have become a businessman.

—And how long does it take you to draw pictures for a story like that? It's a month away, you have the time. In any case, if you haven't finished by the twentieth you can bring your work here, Mario knows not to get in the way.

—Last time he refused to get out of my lap.

—Last time was two years ago.

She reproached me, saying I was wanting both as a father and a grandfather. I responded kindly and assured her that I would watch the child as long as she needed. She asked when I was thinking of coming and I overdid it with my reply. Since my daughter sounded unhappier than usual; since during my hospital stay she'd called at most three or four times; since that indifference of hers seemed her way of punishing me for my own, I promised that I would arrive in Naples a week before the conference, so that the child would get used to my being around. And I added, with false enthusiasm, that I was eager to spend some time being a grandfather, that she could go off, carefree, and that Mario and I would have a great time.

As usual, however, I wasn't able to live up to my promise. The young publisher I was working for hounded me, he wanted to see my progress. And I, who hadn't managed to do much of anything because of my ceaseless convalescence, tried, in haste, to finish a couple of plates. But one morning I started losing blood again and had to rush to the doctor who, though finding everything under control, ordered me to come back for another checkup in a week. And so, between one thing and another, I didn't end up leaving until the 18th of November, after sending the publisher the two plates, which were still in rough shape. I went to the station feeling frustrated and annoyed, my suitcase packed willy-nilly, without even a present for Mario other than two volumes of fairy tales that I myself had illustrated several years before.

It was a journey plagued by cold sweats and the desire to head back to Milan. It was raining and I felt tense. The train sliced through gusts of wind that clouded the window with trembling rivulets of precipitation. I was often scared that the wagons, felled by the storm, would jump the tracks, and I realized that the more one aged, the more it mattered to stay alive. But once I got to Naples, despite the rain and the cold, I felt better. I exited the station, and in a few minutes I reached the corner building I knew well.

2.

Betta welcomed me with a fondness that—at forty, consumed by the balancing act of her days—I didn't think she was capable of. She seemed surprisingly worried about my health, exclaiming: You're so pale, so thin, and she apologized for never visiting me when I was in the clinic. Since she asked about the doctors and the tests with a certain alarm, I suspected she was wondering if she was taking a chance by leaving her child with me. I reassured her and went on to pay her a thousand compliments with the hyperbolic phrases I'd resorted to ever since she was little.

—You look beautiful.

—No I don't.

—You're prettier than a movie star.

—I'm fat, moody, and old.

—Are you kidding? I've never seen a more attractive woman. Sure, the personality's rough as bark, but if you peel it off there's a smooth, sensitive interior, the hue as lovely and luminous as your mother's.

Saverio had gone to get Mario at daycare, they'd be back any minute. I hoped she'd tell me to go to my room for a bit and rest. On the rare occasions I came to Naples, I slept in the big room next to the bathroom with a small balcony that resembled a launching pad over Piazza Garibaldi. I was raised there along with my siblings, and it was the only corner of the house I didn't detest. I'd have liked to hole up and stretch out on the bed for a few minutes. But Betta kept me in the kitchen—me, the suitcase, a cloth bag—and proceeded to complain nonstop about everything: her job at the university, Mario, Saverio who dumped house and child onto her shoulders, and countless other unbearable stressors in her life.

—Dad, she almost shouted at a certain point, I am *totally* fed up.

She was standing next to the sink, washing vegetables, but when she said this she turned toward me with an abrupt, violent twist of her body. For a few seconds I saw her—and this had never happened—as pure suffering matter that her mother and I had lightly, guiltily tossed into the world four decades ago. Actually no, not Ada. My wife had passed away a while back, she no longer bore the responsibility. Betta was a big broken-off cell, mine, only mine, the membrane already pretty worn out. Or at least this was how I imagined her for an instant. Then I heard the sound of the front door. My daughter quickly got hold of herself, saying "here they are" with a combination of joy and repulsion, and Saverio appeared— stocky, ceremonious, broad-faced Saverio, miles from Betta's lanky elegance—along with Mario, tiny, dark-haired like his father, eyes big on his thin face, red hat, blue coat, puffy light-blue pom-poms.

The child, thrilled, was expectant for a few seconds. He didn't get anything from Betta, I thought. He's his father through and through. Meanwhile I felt, with a prick of anguish, that I was the word *grandpa* materializing before him—a stranger from whom he expected a boundless flow of delights—and I opened up my arms somewhat theatrically. Mario, I said, come, sweetheart, come, my, how you've grown. He then threw himself against me and I had to pick him up, speaking joyfully, though my voice was cracking from the strain. He clasped my neck with great force and kissed one of my cheeks as if he wanted to perforate it.

—Not like that, you're choking him, his father said, stepping between us. Betta also put in her two cents right away, ordering him to let me go.

—Grandpa's not going anywhere. You'll be together, just the two of you, for the next few days; you'll share your room with him.

That was awful news for me. I'd imagined that a boy so young slept with his parents. I'd forgotten that I myself had demanded, long ago, that Betta sleep in her crib in the neighboring room, even though Ada couldn't sleep a wink at the thought of not hearing her whimpers or missing a feeding. I remembered it now, just as I was putting the child back on the ground, and I repressed my irritation, I didn't want Mario to perceive it. I went to the cloth bag that I'd leaned up next to my suitcase when I'd arrived and pulled out a couple of slim books that I wanted to give him as a gift.

—Look what I've brought you, I said. But as soon as I touched the books, fearing he'd be disappointed, I once again regretted not having bought him something more enticing. Instead the child took both volumes, eagerly, and softly saying an extremely polite thank you—they were the first words I'd heard him pronounce—proceeded to examine the covers.

Saverio, who, just like me, must have thought that the gift was a mistake and later, surely, would have said to Betta: As usual your father can't do anything right, rushed to exclaim:

—Grandpa's an important artist, look how lovely the drawings are, he did them.

—You'll look at them together, later, Betta said. Now take off your coat and come pee.

Mario put up a small fight but then got undressed, making sure above all to hold on to the two books. He even took them with him when his mother dragged him forcefully into the bathroom. I sat back down, ill at ease, not knowing what to discuss with my son-in-law. I trotted out small talk about the university, students, and the fatigue of teaching. It was the only subject, as far as I recalled, that aroused him other than soccer, which I knew nothing about. But Saverio turned another corner almost immediately and to my surprise—given that we were wary of one another—started to speak in bloated but pained terms about existential frustration.

—There's never a break, there's no happiness, he said quietly.

—There's always a little happiness.

—No, it's all been poisoned.

But the minute Betta returned she put a swift end to our

intimacy and he started to talk again, confusedly, about the university. Obviously the mere sight of one another was enough for husband and wife to get worked up. My daughter accused Saverio of having left something—I didn't understand what exactly—in disarray, and meanwhile reiterated to me, nodding to Mario who had just reappeared clutching my gift: The upshot is that *this guy* is growing up worse than his father. And then, with some vehemence, she took away my suitcase and bag, betting, with a sarcastic chuckle, that it contained everything I needed to work but no shirts, socks, or underwear.

The child seemed relieved when she disappeared down the hallway. He placed one of the books on the table, arranged the other on my legs as if they were a desk, and began to leaf through each page. I ran my hands through his hair and he, perhaps encouraged by the gesture, asked me, composed:

—Did you really draw these pictures, Grandpa?

—I sure did, do you like them?

He thought about it.

—They're a little dark.

—Dark?

—Yes. Next time make them lighter.

Saverio hastened to step in:

—They're not dark, what are you talking about? They're just right.

—They're dark, Mario repeated.

I gently extracted the book from him and examined a few of the illustrations. No one had ever told me they were dark. I turned to the boy and said: They're not dark, and added, a bit piqued: But if you think they're dark, then something's wrong. I leafed carefully through the pages, noting defects that had never occurred to me, and murmured quietly: Maybe they were poorly printed. And my mood soured, I'd never been able to tolerate other people's sloppiness when it spoiled my work. I repeated to Saverio, various times: They're dark, yes,

Mario's right. Then, mixing together complaints about technical details, I proceeded to criticize all publishers who demanded so much, who spent so little, who ruined everything.

For a while the child sat listening. Then he got bored and asked if I wanted to see his toys. But by then my mind was elsewhere and I curtly said no. In an instant I realized the refusal was too harsh; both father and son were already looking at me, bemused. I added: Tomorrow, little guy, Grandpa's tired now.

3.

That evening it finally clicked that the conference in Cagliari was, above all, a prime opportunity for Betta and Saverio to evade the eyes and ears of their child and fight hard. If, in the course of the afternoon, they only rarely spoke to each other, with perfunctory sentences, at dinner they didn't even bother with those. Instead they talked to Mario and to me, so that the boy would know all my exploits and I'd know his. They both carried on in childish voices and almost always started the conversation with *you know that Grandpa* or *show Grandpa how you*. As a result, Mario had to learn that I'd won many prizes, that I was more famous than Picasso, that important people displayed my work in their homes; and I had to learn that Mario knew how to answer the phone politely, write his name, use the remote control, cut his meat with a real knife, and eat what was on his plate without throwing a tantrum.

It was an interminable evening. The whole while the child never took his eyes off me, as if, fearing I would disappear, he wanted to memorize me. When I showed him some dumb old tricks that I'd used to entertain Betta when she was little—like pretending that my thumb, clenched between two fingers, was a piece of his nose I'd snatched away—he hinted at half indulgent little smiles, half amused, striking the air with his hand as if to punish me for such foolishness. When it was time to go to bed, he tried to say: I'll go when Grandpa goes. But both parents stepped in, almost in unison, both suddenly strict. His mother exclaimed: You go to bed when Mommy tells you to go to bed, and his father said: It's time to sleep, indicating the clock on the wall as if his son already knew how to tell time. Mario put up a little resistance then, but all he managed was to make sure I watched how he got undressed without help, and how, still without help, he put on his pajamas, and how he squeezed the toothpaste neatly onto his toothbrush, and how he knew how to brush his teeth, ceaselessly.

I observed the performance, admiring him. I said, an infinite number of times: What a good boy you are, and Betta insisted, also an infinite number of times: Don't spoil him.

—Although, she added, suddenly serious, watching her son: he really is a good boy for his age. You'll see.

At that point mother and son announced that they were withdrawing to read the nightly fairy tale. I followed them without conviction, to the room that was no longer mine. Mario didn't know how to read yet but—Betta emphasized— he was coming along. They both wanted to demonstrate this to me, and indeed the child, with a little help from his mother, read a few words. Meanwhile I threw an eager glance at the folding cot that had been prepared for me and thought that, just to lie down, I, too, would have listened to the fairy tale. Don't go yet, Grandpa, the boy was saying, but Betta held sway over him, saying, No Dad, go, we'll read a little and then it's time for bed. Words that were clearly instructions both for him and for me.

I left the room and turned unwillingly—where was the switch?—down the dark hallway. Already in Milan, in recent years, I wasn't fond of the dark. I would turn on all the lights at home because after my operation, at times, the darkness animated the inanimate, and I'd be under the impression that the furniture or the walls were grabbing me, something I attributed to my poorly circulating blood, to the lack of oxygen going to my brain. I therefore stepped forward prudently, running my knuckles along the walls, but I still saw my father in flashes, grim, throwing his hair back with both his hands, and my mother, who transformed amid fits of terror and melancholy from a shabby Cinderella to a lady in a veiled hat, and my grandmother, who, having suffered a stroke, now sat always silent, *arrugnata*, a word that, in dialect, meant a body folded in on itself, curved like a billhook left to rust in some corner.

The only bright spot in the apartment was the kitchen. There I found my son-in-law, in a foul humor but nevertheless solicitous. He pointed to the seat next to him. I'd barely settled down before he started telling me, in a lowered voice, practically into my ear, how things between him and Betta—two years of dating, twelve living together, five married—had fallen apart. It was useless trying to change the topic, to signal in every way possible that I didn't want to listen. There was nothing connecting us, and I was, moreover, his wife's father, but he carried on, it was clear that he was unhappy and that he wanted to vent. He told me that some guy my daughter knew from high school had come to direct the math department and that she'd fallen for him right away. That brilliant mathematician, a powerful man, had inoculated her with new energy, so much that every day she took the time to look prettier and more elegant than the day before. In short the university had become, for Betta, an enormous container full of a liqueur-like substance within which her thin body floated at every moment, almost without wanting to, toward this hulking new arrival—a massive being, according to Saverio, with fat thighs, a weighty belly—with the objective of brushing against him, bumping into him, then stroking him, getting close to him, dragging him down with her to the bottom.

—Your daughter's doing all this, he whispered, his eyes swollen with desperation, right in front of me.

That's what was unbearable about it, he repeated to me more than once: Betta wasn't even the least bit concerned with hiding how fiercely she was attracted to the director. She sought out contact in the hallways, office, classrooms, in the cafè, never caring about her husband's presence, without giving weight to the fact that, at any moment, he might be there to witness it. Betta, with Saverio, was increasingly, shamelessly excited. She'd ask Saverio, every morning, if she was well dressed, if she was attractive enough. She'd dropped a hiss of uncontrollable jealousy into Saverio's ear when, on a certain occasion, the director had appeared with a wife who clung to his side, not skimping on her affections. Not to mention the languid greetings at the start and end of the work day: kisses on the cheeks that inadvertently tended, always a touch more, to land on the mouth. And this was still not taking into account a furious demand for independence. Once, when Saverio, driven out of his mind by her behavior, had pulled her aside into one of the dark tunnels of the department to yell at her, telling her how she was humiliating him, she'd hollered at him: What's your problem, what are you talking about, you're crazy, I'll do what I want, and she'd left him in the lurch to run to the cafè behind that super-magnet who—my son-in-law made sure to say—if you met him, you'd see that he's little more than an agglomeration of life, the kind that existed before the start of evolution, in brief, a fucking piece of shit.

I didn't say a thing the whole time. I let him vent. It was useless to point out that the director, as described to me, was nothing but a portrait of himself. Useless telling him that evidently the type of man that Betta was attracted to was massive and—like him—nothing to look at. I only tried to toss out, at a certain point: It's just a passing infatuation, Savè, in the end what endures are habits, fondness. And Mario, a marvelous little boy. It would be a shame to torment him with your fighting: Take my advice, let it pass. His reply was instant, like the darting of a snake, and upset me greatly: Yes, he said, this hankering will ebb, she'll calm down; but I—*I've* seen it all, and it revolts me, I don't love her anymore.

I wanted him to elaborate on that point—the nexus between his crazed seeing and the end of love—but hearing Betta's steps in the corridor, stricken with fear, he interrupted himself. My daughter appeared on the threshold in her nightgown. Looking contemptuously at her husband, she announced:

—I'm ready, Dad's tired, let's go to bed. Go brush your teeth while I lock the doors and lower the blinds.

Saverio stared for a second or two at the floor and then, after barely uttering goodnight to me, got up from his chair with a decisive jolt and left. Betta waited to hear the sound of the bathroom door closing, then asked me, anxiously, scarcely audible:

—What did he tell you?

—That you're having some problems.

—He's the problem.

—I gather you're the problem.

—You don't get it, Saverio sees things that aren't there.

—So you're not having an affair with some sort of director?

—Me? *Me?* No way, Dad, Saverio's impossibile.

—But you've been together twenty years.

—I've stayed with him because he's usually balanced in his own way.

—And now he's unbalanced?

—Yes, and now he's throwing everything off balance: me, our son, the house, everything.

—Hold on: He's unbalanced to the degree that he sees you glommed onto a stranger while you, on the other hand, want nothing to do with him?

Betta grimaced in a way that turned her ugly.

—He's not a stranger, Dad. He's a brother to me.

At that point her eyes filled with tears, something that, combined with my general dislike of her husband, rendered her immediately sincere. I told her: Come here, calm down, you're smart, you're wonderful at your job, Mario's a delight, come on, go away together, talk to each other, and when you get back, it will all be OK. But whether or not she was sincere, I knew well enough that I would have loved and consoled her forever. I could never bear it when she cried when she was little, and I couldn't bear it now that she was an adult. If you really have to cry, I whispered to her, cry when I'm in Milan. She smiled, I kissed her forehead, she sniffled and muttered: Let me show you where to shut off the gas. She wasn't satisfied, wanting to see me turn the lever so that I memorized the gesture. Then she went on to give me thousands of instructions: where the switch was for the fuse box, mind the door to the balcony, it was new and didn't work that well, where to turn off the water under the sink, the shower drain backed up sometimes, et cetera. Then she realized that I wasn't paying attention and she said quietly, frustrated, I'll write it all down for you tomorrow. Meanwhile the worry that I couldn't handle the situation that she herself had put me in must have resurfaced, and she asked, staring me straight in the eyes: You're really up to taking care of him? I swore that I was and she kissed me on the cheek—something she never did, not even when she was little, and said softly, thank you.

My gaze followed her until she disappeared into her room. Then I went to get my things out of my suitcase, careful not to make noise, and I locked myself in the bathroom. There, as I prepared myself for the night with slow movements rendered unsteady from fatigue, I thought back to those first hours in Naples, and once again regretted having left Milan. The hell with feeling up to it. I should have made clear that I was still convalescing, and that I couldn't take on the responsibility of Mario, that I didn't want to be burdened by their marital woes. I reinvoked embarrassing sentences and images from the evening and couldn't manage to drive away a certain impression of—how should I put it?—a lack of decorum. It presently struck me that everything in that house lacked the proper attire. Or maybe it wasn't improper, but as if worn by a bituminous magma, or a crocodile, or, who knows, some pygmy chimpanzees, or worse, protocells, lipids, in their initial blind stage of aggregation. Betta kissing up to her colleague lacked decorum; and the husband wedged between her and the stranger—a lover, a brother, a brotherly lover—lacked decorum; how lacking in decorum were the walls, the breeze that blew in from the marina, the city. Following my wife's death, I'd looked through her papers—I, too, lacking in decorum—and it only took me a short while to realize that, while I was distracted day and night by small petty trials in order to affirm myself as an artist—and there had been many years of distraction, so many, during which what had counted most was cultivating my own whims—she had often betrayed me, even a few years after we'd become a couple. Why? She didn't explain herself, either, she only guessed. To remember that she was there. To give herself some centrality. Because my centrality, within our relationship, was excessive. Because her body needed attention. Because her vitality had taken a blind leap. Behind our decorous day-to-day life—I sighed, full of discontent—there's a wild, uncouth sprite we pretend not to see: an energy that animates our flesh, thoroughly crushing, at fixed intervals, the composure even of extremely composed people. I turned off the bathroom light, and the one in the hallway—three switches, I pressed one at random, it was the right one—after turning on the lamp at my bedside. And finally I lay down, with a long stifled groan, without even casting a glance at Mario and the other end of the room, with his toddler bed among a sea of toys and countless drawings pinned to the walls.

Outside, a ferocious wind continued to blow. The rain was beating against the platform of the balcony, the railing shook, and the sound invaded the room in spite of the double-paned glass. I fell asleep at once, but the next instant I was already awake, in a sweat, my breath cut off. Mario was beside me in his bright blue pajamas. He said: You forgot to turn off the light, Grandpa, but I'll turn it off for you, don't worry. He really did turn it off, and darkness and wind overtook the room, terrifying me. He slipped away, unafraid, to his bed.

4.

I woke up convinced that it was four-twenty, the exact time, give or take a minute, that my sleep terminated in Milan. Gusts of rain still fell. I turned on the lights; it was two-ten. I pulled myself up to go to the bathroom and the warmth I'd been enjoying under the covers gave way to a shudder of cold air. On my way back I glanced at Mario, who'd tossed off the covers in his sleep. He lay on his stomach, his legs splayed, an arm stretched along one side, the other folded with his hand clenched in a fist next to his half-open mouth. His bare feet, when I brushed them with my hand, were icy. What if he got sick while his parents were away? I pulled the covers up to his face and went to sit on the edge of my bed.

I felt sluggish. I was sleepy and yet certain that, were I to lay down, I wouldn't sleep: I was too hot under my skin, which, paradoxically, seemed cold to the touch; my toes were also cold and somewhat numb. I took the James story and some pencils out of my suitcase to knock out a few sketches, then I got back under the covers, leaning my back against the wall. I looked over the work I'd done in the preceding weeks and didn't like any of it; on the contrary, I regretted sending the publisher two plates that hadn't even been touched up. I reread a few passages in the book and tried to pin down an image or two. But I couldn't concentrate. It was as if Mario's breath, combined with the breath of the wind and the rain, and the reality of the room—in the apartment Betta and Saverio had adapted to their needs, renovating it over the years—all blocked my imagination. So I set the story aside and abandoned myself to a state of half-sleep in which the memory of the old arrangement of the house assumed a precision capable of making any other image, either real or imagined, fade. I pulled myself up again and started to draw the spaces in which I'd been raised. I drew the entryway with the window that looked over the freight yard. I drew the living room that meant so much to my mother, with furniture that had just been bought, the sofa, the armchairs, the ottomans, things that must have been the height of elegance to her. I drew her, too, and then immediately afterward—I thought I could do it—her gaze upon that bright, wide space, upon the table with its wavy border, the silverware with its rounded tips and four tines, the gallery from which you could see part of the Hotel Terminus. I drew the hallway with the telephone unit nailed to the wall, my parents' room, the two of them in bed, my father seated on the edge in his T-shirt and underwear. And I drew the storage room full of old stuff, the enormous bathroom, the room, in that very moment, that I was sharing with Mario. Back then it was full of military beds, like a dormitory in the barracks. My grandmother slept on one, and we five children, head to toe, on the others, an encampment then partially vacated. The room was soon turned over to my grandmother and her three youngest grandchildren, while my brother and I—the two elder grandchildren—went on to make our beds, in the evenings, in the living room, putting an end to my mother's elegant aspirations.

It was frenetic work. It had been a while since my hand was so loose. I drew spaces and people and objects from memory, also reproducing, in a sort of aside—at the top of the page, at the bottom, and on fresh pages—details, details, details. While I'd boasted of a certain capacity throughout my adolescence—and it slowly had imposed some direction on my life: The drawing teacher in middle school was astonished, saying, this boy is self-taught—later, growing up, studying, the talent of my body, hand, and nerves seemed unrefined. I pursued increasingly cultivated choices and, as a result, increasingly distanced myself from talents that seemed vulgar to me by then. When I was twelve, other people thought I was a prodigy who dazzled and disturbed, and I myself felt that way; but by the time I was twenty I'd learned to deride the facility of my hands as if it were a weakness. I saw myself, I imagined myself, I tried to draw myself in those two ages, at twelve and at twenty. But abruptly my hand cramped up. I kept at it in vain, my fingers again turning heavy and subordinate. I scribbled a while longer, words, sketches: how I was, who I was, what had happened during those eight years in which I had fully grown up. Around four in the morning I stopped. How foolish, wasting time this way. What was it all for? I looked over the sheets crammed with drawings, stunned by that unexpected eruption of creativity. And I was struck, in that throng of images, by two figures who were all too precise: Betta and Saverio. Betta had turned out marvelously. I'd put her into the kitchen sixty years ago, in a pose my mother often struck, as did I. She resembles you and your family, Ada used to say. Even though she'd been the one to give birth to her, even under those circumstances, I'd excluded her. My son-in-law on the other hand, a perfect likeness, in the kitchen as it was today—with scant references—was dull. I'd portrayed him as a surly stranger, I'd erased, unwittingly, all positive traits. I turned off the light, pulled the covers up to my face, and at the hour when, normally, in Milan, I woke up, fell asleep.

5.

But I didn't sleep much. I awoke around six. No more wind, maybe it had stopped raining, too. When I stepped into the hallway I hit the wrong switch and turned on the lights in the room. I shut them off right away, hoping the child wouldn't wake up, and went to shave and wash my face.

I meanwhile hoped that Betta might have gotten up, roused by the noise I made, but even when I came out of the bathroom the house was perfectly quiet. I went to the kitchen. I struggled to locate a saucepan that seemed fit to boil water, but there was no tea. I didn't know what to do in front of the burner. Where were the matches? Or the lighter? I was standing there immobile, stuck, when Mario appeared at my side, his face still sleepy.

—Hi, Grandpa.

—Did I wake you?

—Yes.

—Sorry.

—It doesn't matter. Can I give you a kiss?

—Yes, give me a kiss.

I saw that he had sensibly put a little orange woolen jacket over his pajamas, and slippers of the same color on his feet. I praised him and bent down to let him kiss me, and to kiss him in return.

—Can I smack my lips?

—Okay.

He smacked his lips hard against my cheek and then asked me, in Saverio's formal way, if I needed anything.

—Do you know how to turn on the gas? I asked.

He nodded yes. First off he reminded me that there was the knob to turn, and though it was obvious I'd already turned it, he wanted nevertheless to explain how it was done: This way, see, there's no gas, but if you turn it, it comes out. Then he dragged a chair over to me, informing me beforehand that it wouldn't make noise: Dad glued little felt pads under the legs of all the chairs. Then he nimbly clambered up and explained the symbols designed to indicate the appropriate flame. But the thing that really amazed me—and also alarmed me—was that he knew how to use the burners: He pressed a knob, he turned it, intently he watched the sparks until they burst into flame. He waited a few seconds and let go of the knob.

—See that? he said, satisfied.

—Yes, but I'll put the pan on.

—Aren't we making breakfast for everyone?

—I don't know what you have, what your mom and dad have.

—I do. Mom and Dad have coffee with milk and I just have milk.

—Then?

—Then you have to toast bread for Mom—Dad and I eat biscuits—and squeeze oranges for everyone. Want some juice?

—No.

—It's good.

—I don't want any.

He proceeded to show me where the oranges were, where the juicer was, how to toast the bread so that it wouldn't burn and emanate a foul odor that disgusted his father, which shelf held the bags of black tea and green, which cupboard contained the coffeepots, where the teapot was since the saucepan I'd chosen was inadequate, where the placemats were for setting the table. Oh, the quantity of things he said that morning, and with such command. At a certain point he asked me, worried:

—Did you check the expiration on the milk?

—No, but if it's in the fridge, surely it's good.

—You still have to check, Mom forgets sometimes.

—You check, I said, teasing him.

He smiled, embarrassed, striking the air the way he had the previous evening, and admitted reluctantly:

—I don't know how to check.

—So there is something you don't know how to do.

—I know that you have to put a little milk in a saucepan, turn on the gas and see if it curdles.

—Curdles? What does it mean, to curdle?

He lowered his eyes, turning red, and looked up at me again with a crooked smile. He was anxious, he couldn't bear falling flat on his face. Jump, I said, grabbing his hand and letting him jump off the chair. Then, to convince him that I still gave him credit, I asked: What else do we need to do? I was amazed—I'm not sure I was amused, maybe not amused—by his incredible vocabulary and by how in command he was. I, as far as I knew, from what my mother and grandmother had told me, had been practically mute and always absentminded. Imagination prevailed over a sense of reality; even as an adult I'd never known how to participate actively in the practical side of life. The only thing I really knew how to do was draw and paint, combining all kinds of colored materials. Beyond this realm I had little intelligence, little memory. I cherished few desires and paid little heed to the responsibilities of civilian life. I always trusted others, Ada above all. This child, on the other hand, though barely four years old, displayed an attention to the world as keen as the Indians who learned complex techniques from goldsmiths who'd arrived with the Conquistadors, simply by observing them. He guided me step by step. Following his orders, I set the kitchen table. Next he showed me the coffee: Betta drank decaf, Saverio no. Then together we prepared the coffeepots, together we used the juicer, and he scolded me more than once for my tendency to throw out the orange halves when the pulp around the edges was still full of juice. *Together* almost always meant that even the actions he lacked the strength or ability to perform had to be performed by putting his hands on top of mine, and if I tended to exclude him, he turned sulky.

—Was it your mother who taught you to do all this?

—Dad. He never does anything alone, I always have to help.

—And Mom?

—Mom's jittery, she yells and goes fast.

—Has Dad told you never to turn on the gas?

—Why?

—Because you can burn yourself.

—If you know you can get burned, be careful and you won't get burned.

—You can get burned even if you're careful. Promise me that as long as we're together, you'll never turn on the gas without me.

—When you're here I won't get burned?

—No.

—What if you get burned?

He wanted to assuage my fears in case this were to happen. He told me there was a box with a red cross on the lid, in the bathroom. Inside was a useful cream because the times that he'd gotten a burn his father had spread it on him so that the pain went away.

—It's not sticky, he reassured me, and precisely at the point when I couldn't take it anymore—entertain him, sure, but I was starting to feel trapped by that instruction-manual voice of his—Betta turned up. I breathed a sigh of relief. Oh my goodness, my daughter exclaimed, pretending to be thrilled by the table set before her.

—Grandpa and I did everything.

She lavished the child with praise and gathered him up in her arms. She smothered his neck with kisses, tickling him, making him laugh.

—It's fun being with Grandpa, huh?

—Yes.

Betta turned to me:

—And you like being with Mario, Dad?

—Very much.

—Thank goodness you decided to come.

In the meantime Saverio also showed up, and the child immediately turned on the burners—causing no one to worry—under the coffee, decaf and regular. I put a couple of bags into the boiling teapot and finally we proceeded to have a breakfast nothing like the solitary, frugal breakfasts I had every morning in Milan. There wasn't a moment's silence. The two parents—even more hostile toward one another—did nothing but encourage the ongoing chitchat of their son. But as soon as we finished Betta announced that she had to run and get ready, she had a busy day and—she complained—she still had to pack, she hadn't thought about what to wear in Cagliari, and the following day they would have to get up at four, given that the flight was at nine. But—she said—I made you a list of things you need to deal with once we've left, make sure you remember, Dad. Then she went out pulling Mario behind her, since he had to wash and get dressed for school, but all the while he kept saying: I don't want to go, I want to stay with Grandpa.

I gingerly asked Saverio:

—Will I have to take Mario to nursery school, the next few days?

—You have to ask your daughter, she hasn't told me anything.

—Maybe you should trust her more. You're too suspicious, it aggravates her.

—How can I not be suspicious if she behaves the way she behaves? You know where she's going this morning?

—You tell me.

—To read her article to that son of a bitch.

—What's wrong with that?

—Nothing. But then explain why he hasn't asked to meet with me, why he hasn't asked to read my paper, too?

—You haven't been friends since high school, for one thing.

—So it's because they're friends that he's asked Betta to give one of the introductory talks, while I've been scheduled the second day?

I looked at him, confused.

—This director has something to do with the conference in Cagliari?

—He has everything to do with it. He organized it.

—And he'll be there with you?

—You didn't know?

I didn't have time to comment. Betta, irate, called her husband from the bathroom. You need to take Mario to nursery—she shouted at him, exasperated, practically running down the hallway leaving a trail of perfume—are you pretending to forget? Saverio got up with a start, and I watched him slip away, discombobulated. According to Betta her husband was a mathematician of a certain stature, but I couldn't believe that a person with an organized mind could behave so coarsely. Let's even assume that Betta really does have some feelings for this director, I thought. Is Saverio so stupid as to think he can prevent those feelings from turning into something else? Sexual pleasure, uncoupled once and for all from reproduction, which was its original purpose, continuously leaked fluids all over the planet, in every season. And there was no controlling it, whatever had to happen would happen no matter what;

it was the careening force of bodies that ruthlessly wiped out wives, husbands, children, affections, economies. Betta reappeared. At eight-thirty in the morning she was gussied up as if she were off to the disco. She pushed Mario in front of me, perfectly combed, he elegant in his own way, ready for nursery school.

—Grandpa, my daughter commanded, tell Mario that he has to go to school today.

I assumed a solemn air:

—Mario, don't complain now, you have to go.

—I want to stay with you.

Betta sputtered:

—Enough with what you want. From now on you are to do everything Grandpa tells you.

She kissed her son on the head, said goodbye to me, and disappeared. The child repeated, looking me up and down:

—I'm not going to nursery.

6.

Mario stuck to his guns, trying, with that look of his, to get me to agree. His father said neither yes nor no, he merely dragged him off, they were both terribly late. Grandpa, the boy said softly, depressed as he got into the elevator. Don't leave, wait for me here. I nodded yes and shut the door, relieved.

I wandered reluctantly through the empty apartment, mentally comparing the spaces I'd drawn during the night with what the house had now become. The huge living room was half its previous size, the other half had become a study with an aggressively modern desk and floor-to-ceiling shelves. Work had been done on the foyer, too. I hadn't noticed it when I'd arrived, but it now occurred to me that they'd built a new wall with a shiny new door. I opened it and stepped into a small area, also filled with books, but with an old-fashioned desk and an incongruous smell of garlic, onions, and detergent. I opened up the old window that gave onto a small terrace, which—I discovered—had been modified as well. Now it was a veranda where my daughter stockpiled everything she needed to cook with: the smell of garlic, onions, and detergent came from there. I had no doubt that the bigger space was Betta's and that Saverio worked in the cramped nook.

I went back to the hallway and poked around in the bedroom. It was a huge mess. The dresses my daughter must have tried on and discarded in the process of choosing the one she thought made the best impression looked like shriveled peels on the unmade bed. When my mother and father occupied that room it had seemed enormous to me, but now that Betta had introduced two massive wardrobes as tall as the ceiling and a bed so wide that whoever slept on it must have felt alone, it seemed to have shrunk.

I looked around, I leafed through the books on the bedside table, I stepped onto the balcony. There I was assaulted by the usual roar of traffic. The wind had died down, the sky was dark and still. It was no longer raining. I recognized the long row of contiguous buildings that originated at Piazza Garibaldi. For a few seconds I watched the pedestrians on the sidewalk below and the long line of cars that were advancing toward the marina. When I realized that I'd inadvertently soaked the elbows of my pullover on the railing, I went back inside.

That reconnaissance had sufficed to see that, excluding the living room, where there was a large painting of mine with masses of red and blue, most of the works and small pieces I'd given my daughter over the years weren't on display. Who knew where she and her husband had hidden them. Saverio had always pretended to have high opinions of my work, but my daughter never made the effort to give me any credit. And after all, what credit was there to give, there was nothing more unstable. In recent years no one paid attention to me, not as they once had, too many things had changed. Never mind, I told myself, what did it matter, the important thing was that I was still working. I beat back my melancholy and decided to take a walk, given that from tomorrow, because of the child, it would no longer be possible. So I went back to Mario's room, which was still dark. I put on my coat, got my hat, and checked to make sure I had my wallet and, most importantly, the keys that Betta had given me, making me swear that I would never forget them. She was right, things slipped my mind, I had to pay attention. I had the urge to complete my exploration of the house and look at the balcony, so I lifted up the shutters.

It was a place that used to frighten my mother. She would approach it carefully and didn't want my younger siblings to go there alone. I opened the brand-new glass door. The balcony was anomalous, all the balconies on that side were. They were shaped like a trapezoid, tapering as they thrust over the void. Ours was on the top floor, the sixth, and maybe this was why my mother, who normally didn't suffer from vertigo, poorly withstood the effect of that tapering, saying that if she looked down she felt sick. When something needed to be taken in or out she would call my father, and if my father wasn't there, or cranky, she called me, the eldest child. I'd get her what she needed, but then unexpectedly I'd leap to the far end of the balcony and I'd start to jump, causing the platform and the railing to vibrate, and look at her, framed by the doorway, while she laughed and was terrified at the same time.

I liked that semblance of risk. When I was a boy I used to sit on the balcony especially in spring, settling down to read, to write, to draw. The sky had been huge, I remembered, and you could see the spires of the new station. There, over that expanse, I felt like a guard in a tower or a sentinel at the top of a majestic tree, waiting for the sight of something unknown.

But that morning, when I put my head out, I no longer felt the same pleasure. If anything, I felt my mother's anxiety. The balcony was a long thin slab over the gray patch of asphalt; venturing onto it felt like placing my feet on a shard about to fly off the building. Maybe—I said to myself—it's the trapezoidal shape that suggests an unwarranted overhang: The sound, straight line that runs along the glass door feels so far from the parallel version that slices into the void; or more likely it's the weak state I'm in, it's old age, that makes me feel insecure and exposed. Needless to say I stood prudently on the threshold, wearing my coat, holding my hat, looking at the sky, the railing that dripped bright drops of rain, and a plastic bucket with a few toys poking out of it, a cord tied to its handle.

—Your cell phone's ringing, a woman's voice said behind my shoulders, making me shudder. As I turned around, abruptly, imagining my grandmother's ghost, or my mother's, or Ada's, the voice added: Sorry, I'm Sally.

She was the cleaning lady. My cell phone, which I'd probably forgotten in the kitchen, buzzed in the hand she extended toward me. I guessed she was over sixty. She had a full cheerful face and big eyes. She apologized over and over again for having frightened me: She had keys and had come in like every other morning, not thinking that it might scare me.

—You didn't scare me, you surprised me, I clarified.

—Fear, surprise, it's all the same.

—No, it's not the same.

I took the phone that kept buzzing. It was the publisher. He said lightly:

—I got the two plates.

I nudged him toward a positive review.

—They turned out well, don't you think?

For a few seconds, silence. I'd always been used to receiving compliments, for whatever I did. Then, as I grew older, I took them for granted, for it was unlikely that someone would tell me, brutally: No, you've done a terrible job. But I hadn't taken into account the fact that I was talking to an enterprising thirty-year-old, filthy rich. The publisher said:

—I'm not seeing what I was expecting.

—Well then, I said, pretending to be amused, look a little harder.

—I looked carefully, we need to rework this.

I froze. I wanted to react but it seemed ridiculous to insist that the plates were wonderful. I didn't think they were, either. I let him talk. And he talked at length, he talked about vibrancy, believing it was the word that expressed the indispensable quality of the deluxe volume he had in mind. I struggled to understand, it seemed he was talking about colors. But when I asked him to better explain himself, it emerged that my illustrations lacked vibrancy, as if they were short on oxygen.

—Please don't take it the wrong way, he said. But there's no energy here, no intelligence.

I decided to joke with him in a fatherly way.

—If you want me to administer more oxygen to the drawings, I'll try.

This irked him.

—Great, OK, give them more oxygen. Your way of putting it may amuse you but it seems serious and right to me. Where do the others stand?

—They're coming along well, I lied.

He wasn't appeased. He said a deluxe edition demanded an enormous effort, that a number of highly competent people were already on the job, that he needed the material as soon as possible. He was young, and he thought that speaking aggressively turned him authoritative. I lied to him in greater detail and put an end to the conversation. Only then did I realize that my hands were burning, and that my back was covered with sweat. He hadn't liked the plates, and this vexed me. But what vexed me even more was that the young man had told me so, bluntly. I put the cell phone back into my pocket, I felt a headache coming on. I didn't like the fact that Sally was sitting on my bed taking off a shoe, and she realized it.

—They're new, they hurt, she explained, quickly putting it on again and standing up.

—I'm going out for a walk, I said.

—OK. Happy about your grandson?

—Yes.

—You don't come down often.

—I come when I can.

—Such a sweetheart, little Mario. But now and then he needs a scolding. Look at this mess, he's even left his toys outside, they've been there for days.

She sighed heavily and excused herself to the balcony. She was a small but heavy woman. I was tempted to say, forget about it, don't go out there. But she clearly didn't share my anxiety. She moved toward the bucket even though the balcony vibrated under her feet. She pulled the toys out of the bucket and threw the rain that had collected at the bottom over the balcony.

—They make him play outside even when it's cold, she complained.

—They grow up nice and strong that way.

—You're kidding, bravo, grandparents need to kid around, make them laugh. But they need to worry a little, too.

I replied that I was worried, above all, about the days I had to spend alone with Mario, that I had a lot of work to do.

—What are your hours? I asked.

—Nine to noon. But I'm not coming day after tomorrow.

—You're not coming?

—I have to see someone, it's important.

—Does my daughter know?

—Sure she knows. What should I cook?

—I leave it to you.

Now, in addition to feeling embittered because of the publisher's rudeness, I was mad at Betta. She'd told me—or at any rate she'd led me to believe—that Sally would come every day. But this wasn't the case. I closed the glass door. Even with my coat on, I felt cold. Someone pressed the buzzer once, twice, three times. Pressing lengthily, repeatedly, urgently.

7.

It was Saverio. Sally ran downstairs without explaining a thing to me and reappeared soon after with Mario, who was beaming.

—Dad brought me back home, he said.

—Why?

—The teacher was sick.

—And there wasn't another teacher?

—I don't want to stay with another teacher, I want to stay with you.

—How did you manage to convince your father?

—I cried.

I asked Sally if I could leave him with her for an hour, I had a problem at work and I needed to think. She replied that her time was limited, that it was a big house, and that what would really make her happy was if Grandpa and grandson both went for a walk until lunchtime.

How to respond? I told Mario to put down his backpack and come with me. The boy was eager. Sally told him:

—Go pee-pee, my little Mario: Before going out you always need to go pee-pee. Right, Grandpa?

We went out, where the wind was freezing. I put up my collar, pulled my hat over my head, and wrapped the scarf around the child's neck. After all that I intoned, so that he understood that I wasn't going to budge:

—Mario, let's make one thing clear. I'm not going to carry you.

—Okay.

—And don't ever let go of my hand, for any reason.

—Got it.

—Is there something special you'd like to do?

—Let's ride the new subway.

We headed off toward Piazza Garibaldi, but after walking for a bit I wasn't crazy about Mario's idea. The piazza, the hub of the station, was a dense network of people in a hurry, vendors of every possibile item, layabouts, cars, busses. The entrance to the subway was also crowded. The idea of sinking down into it was unbearable, I needed air. I decided to turn back.

—Grandpa, the subway's that way.

—I'll show you the way I used to walk to school.

—You said we'd ride the subway.

—You said that, not me.

I needed to take a long walk and forget the publisher's voice. But the latter wasn't easy to do. Again I analyzed the phone call in my head, trying to identify some saving grace. I told myself: Given that he didn't like the two attempts I'd made, I could change course without much trouble, since the work was still at an early stage. But then right away I objected: Change course in order to go where? It was likely that I really had produced bad work. It was likely the low hemoglobin, the ferratin, the forced departure that had prevented me from doing my best. But what about respect? Those two plates were part of my story, part of who I was, what I'd done successfully for decades. If that presumptuous boy had commissioned the work, if he'd said: Illustrate this James, it was because of my name, for everything I'd produced in the course of my life. So what was he expecting? And meanwhile, what did I mean when I said: I still have time to change course? There was only one course, the one I'd trodden from age twenty to seventy-five. Sure, I could improve the two plates, but they stemmed from that path: and only within the confines of that path, consisting of scores of appreciated works, would I be able to retouch them.

I stuffed my hands into my pockets, embittered. I went toward the marina, my head bent down. But Mario yanked me:

—Grandpa, you let go of my hand.

—You're right, I'm sorry.

—This street's ugly, Dad and I never walk down it.

—Even better, that way you get to see new places.

It was the space of my adolescence: alleyways, streets, squares, whirling gullies among the millions of cars on the Forcella, the Duchessa, the Lavinaio, the Carmine, down to the port and the sea, a vast zone continuously streaked by an onrush of local voices—the chitchat of pedestrians, shouts from the windows, exchanges on the thresholds of shops—that resounded tenderly and violently, that were polite and obscene, melding far-apart times: the old me, now, with the child, joined to the time I'd been a boy. Saverio—I knew it even though he'd never told me—had been pressing for years to change neighborhoods; he wanted to convince Betta to sell the apartment and buy another in a part of the city more suited to their professorial lives. I'd told my daughter to sell however and whenever she wanted to, it had been many years since I'd belonged to those streets, that city. But she was tied to Naples, and unlike me she loved that house, or maybe more precisely, loved the memory of her mother.

—Here, I said to the child, pointing to a lowered grate crammed with obscene graffiti, when I was little there used to be a fat lady, enormous, who would fry *graffe*. You know what they are?

—Donuts with sugar.

—Bravo. Sometimes I'd buy one and eat it sitting on those steps.

—Were you as little as me?

—I was twelve.

—You were big, then.

—I don't know.

—It's true, Grandpa, you were big: *I'm* little.

We walked quite a ways. We went toward Sant'Anna alle Paludi and then toward Porta Nolana. The child tried first to stop at every store of Chinese knickknacks, at every parked motorcycle or scooter that he wanted to examine, to show me how powerful they were. But since I pulled him away without paying attention, he ended up walking ahead of me in silence. I was the one, once or twice, who spoke to him, but only to remind myself that he was there, that I was holding his hand. The rest of the time I kept turning over the publisher's words in my head, and since whatever positive spin I could give felt increasingly flimsy, the initial irritation turned to rage. That word was frowned upon in school; teachers and professors would correct us. Not rage—they would scold—we say ire, rabid dogs rage. But the Neapolitan that was spoken in Vasto, at the Pendino, at the Market—the neighborhoods where I was raised, and before that my father and grandparents and great-grandparents, maybe all my ancestors put together—didn't know the word ire, the wrath of Achilles and others who lived in books. They only knew *'a raggia*, rage. The people in this city, I thought, in these neighborhoods and squares and streets and alleyways and stalls by the port filled with toil and illegal loading and unloading, got enraged, they didn't grow irate. They raged at home, on the street, above all when they wandered in search of money and didn't find it. And often it didn't take much to maul others in a rage. *La raggia*, yes, rage, to hell with ire. Did you grow irate? Did you and he? Did they? Give me a break. Teachers and professors gave us a vocabulary that was useless on those streets. It was a city full of dogs, and ire had nothing to do with my bloodshot eyes as I roamed streets like the one we were turning onto now, that led to Garibaldi Way. When I would get out of school and didn't want to go home because I was furious with classmates who tormented me, with sadistic teachers, it was rage that split my chest, my eyes, my head, and to calm myself down I'd take the long way, I'd go down to Porta Nolana, sometimes I went up Via San Cosmo. Other times, when my blood wouldn't stop boiling, I'd go down Lavinaio, I'd go to the Carmine, I'd walk, wild, through blighted neighborhoods, until I reached the port. And if someone bumped into me on the street there was trouble, I swore saints and madonnas up and down, *not* irate *but* in a rage, and I'd laugh mockingly, then spit, I'd throw punches hoping to receive them in return. No one who knows me today would think it, but that's exactly how I was. How lovely it would be—I said to myself—to return to Milan and after half a century reemerge as I'd been as an adolescent, march straight, without stopping, onto Corso Genova, enter the building where the publishing house has its offices, go up to the third floor and without preamble spit in the face of that ill-mannered upstart who criticized my work without respect: not just those illustrations, no, but the work of a lifetime. A pity that the season of rage had died. I'd smothered it long ago.

—Do you know what *'a raggia* means? I asked Mario.

—You shouldn't talk like that, Grandpa.

—Who says that, Dad?

—No, Mom.

—She's right, indeed, you shouldn't talk like that.

—Can I tell you something?

—You can say whatever you like.

—My throat feels a little dry.

—Are you tired?

—Yeah, I'm really tired.

—And what do you do, when you're tired and your throat feels dry?

—You tell me.

—A fruit juice?

We slipped into the first café we saw, a place without light, not even an electric one. It was a small room that smelled neither of coffee nor sweet things to eat but of filth and cigarettes, and I struggled to adjust my eyes. Looking around in search of a couple of chairs, I only saw one round table, made of metal, a few centimeters from the bar. Behind it was a very thin man in his forties with an extremely receding hairline who was reorganizing a grimy shelf. I said: We'd like a fruit juice and a coffee, but we need to sit down because we're tired. And I pointed to the table without chairs. The man perked up suddenly and yelled: Tití, a couple of chairs for the gentleman. A young girl from the back appeared with two chairs made of metal and plastic. I sat down immediately, and Mario climbed onto his. The young girl said: Man, you're pale, and she offered me a glass of water. I took a sip and thanked her.

—What juice would you like? I asked Mario.

He thought hard about it, then said:

—Apple.

—What a cutie, the young girl said.

The words in dialect belonged to me and they were also a sequence of strange sounds. The man and the young girl used them kindly, almost sweetly, but the underlying tone was tantamount to violence. Only in this city—I thought—were people so genuinely inclined to come to your aid and so ready to slit your throat. I no longer knew how to be either aggressive or polite according to Neapolitan standards. The cells within me must have expelled fragments of fury like toxic waste in deeply secluded places, and at a certain point what prevailed was a distant kindness, entirely unlike the one expressed both by the man, who immediately made me a coffee, and by the girl, who served it to me on a tray along with the child's juice, as if between the table and the bar there were a conspicuous distance, and that I myself were unable to take the cup, the glass, by reaching out my hand.

—Grandpa.

—Yes?

—There's no straw.

The girl returned to the back room—I pictured it as a gloomy grotto that led to the foundations of the building—and soon reappeared with the straw. Mario started to sip up his juice, and I drank my coffee. It was good, and after many years I had the urge to smoke a cigarette. That unexpected desire whetted my vision. I saw the packs of cigarettes lined up on a shelf; the man also sold tobacco. I asked for a pack of MS and a box of matches. He passed the cigarettes and the matches to the girl and the girl passed them to me.

—Smoke, the man said, invitingly, addressing me formally, with open arms.

—No thanks, I'll smoke outside.

—Nothing better than a smoke after coffee.

—True.

—So smoke.

—No, thanks again, but no.

I felt like drawing the man, and his gesture of kindhearted permission, so I pulled out a magic marker and a notepad. I'd have liked to say to the publisher, from afar, from the dark depths of the city where I was born: This is the way I live, how dare you find fault. I drew quickly, as if I feared that the man, the girl, the café would dissolve, or that I would dissolve. Mario, slurping on his straw, leaned over to look at what I was doing, and the girl also came close, calling out with unexpected joy:

—Dad, come here.

The father left the bar, looked at the drawing, and said in an Italian as halting as it was embarrassing:

—You are very good.

Mario stepped in:

—My grandfather is a famous artist.

—Indeed, said the man, adding: I knew how to draw, too, then it passed.

I looked at him, confused. It struck me that he'd spoken about his penchant as if it were an illness. I closed the notepad. What had permitted me to escape the city, to feel myself increasingly removed, for good or for ill, from people just like this man, from this setting, when actually, in spite of our age difference, he and I had surely known a similar childhood and adolescence? And then there was the girl. She must have been the same age as Mena, whom I'd loved years ago, before these streets—she used to live nearby—snatched her up forever. For months, she and I had been happy. Then one evening Mena kissed me long and hard, and said she didn't want to see me anymore. I'd already begun to shun how I should be, how they'd taught us to be. I drew and painted, and, thanks to that ability, I was pulling away without realizing it. And in pulling away, instead of appealing to her more, I'd become as bothersome as if my skin had erupted in purple welts. So many airs because I made little pictures, because I thought I'd become someone? You don't even have your license, she'd told me a few days before, you can't take me anywhere, and even though you live in a nice house, your mother can't manage to buy you a new pair of shoes, sometimes she can't even put food on the table because your father gambles away his paycheck.

She was right. My father was known throughout the neighborhood for this, he gambled every last thing, and not to win—he rarely won—but simply for what he called the thrill of the cards slowly revealed, savored at his fingertips, or glanced askew, gimleted: trying to mold live shifting matter according to desire and expectation, almost reinventing it. I'd hated that man. My entire youth and adolescence were a permanent struggle to find a way to rupture the hereditary chain. I wanted to find my own trait, mine alone, that would allow me to shirk his blood. And I'd found it in the ability to recreate almost anything with a pencil. But when I'd shown that skill to Mena, first she'd been amazed, but then she started to deride me. She'd say: You think turning us—me, everyone—into puppets—makes you better than we are? And like that, quickly, she met boys who had a license and a car all to themselves on Saturdays. You're too closed in on yourself, you're patronizing—she told me, and she left.

I waited for Mario to finish his juice but it was clear that he didn't want it anymore, because now instead of drawing it up with his straw he blew out making it bubble up with an unpleasant sound, and smiled at intervals, watching to see if I approved of his exploits. That's enough, I told him. I paid, leaving the girl a tip.

—It's too much, she protested, throwing an inquisitive glance at her father.

—The coffee was good, I said.

—So was the juice, Mario added.

—Thank you, the man said on behalf of his daughter, and I felt that he was looking at me with hostility, as if, just when I was paying and leaving a tip, I was secretly robbing him of something.

Outside there was now a little blue between the bright white clouds, but the wind had picked up again. I extracted a cigarette from the pack as the child watched me, astonished.

—You shouldn't smoke, Grandpa.

—Grandpa's old, he does what he wants.

What a wonderful smell. When Mena still desired me I knew how to beat the wind with matches as she watched, admiringly. In a flash I would pass the flame, still weak, inside the shelter of my palm and the matchbox. I could do it before the wind killed the flame. I tried to do it now. I struck the match against the glossy side of the box but the flicker died instantly, I didn't manage to bring it to the cigarette in time. I

tried again and again. Mario watched me. I had to duck into a
doorway in order to light it. This was another thing that had
vanished: I'd lost the coordination of my movements, I'd lost
my confidence. For a few moments I felt like an insignificant
part of a long process of disintegration, a scale soon destined
to join the organic and inorganic matter solidifying since the
Paleozoic era on the ground and at the bottom of the sea.

—Should we go back home? the boy asked.

—Tired?

—Yes.

—Was nursery school better than Grandpa?

—No.

—Well then?

He looked up at me with a pained expression.

—Can you carry me?

—Don't even think about it.

—But I'm tired, my feet hurt.

—I'm tired too, and my knee hurts.

—But I have a pain going up and down my leg.

We dueled I for I: I, I, I, so energetic and yet so like a feeble chirping, one out, another ahead. I picked up Mario making sure he knew that in five minutes I'd be putting him down
on the ground again. He'd appreciated the books but he
hadn't liked the drawings. They're dark, he'd said, next time
make them lighter. And unlike the publisher, he'd talked that
way not about the illustrations I'd made halfheartedly a few
days before, but about images from years back, work that
meant a lot to me, that had been highly praised. I believed him,
even though I'd always considered those small books success-
ful. Everything crumbles in a few seconds, opinions, certain-
ties. Maybe, I thought, my illustrations no longer speak to a
child.

8.

We found the apartment neat as a pin thanks to Sally's efforts. The kitchen table was already set for two, and we ate what she'd prepared for us. I was tempted to sleep a little. I was incredibly tired, I'd carried Mario in my arms for quite a while and convincing him that I wouldn't be able to make it all the way home had been taxing. But as soon as I tried to stretch out on the bed, the child arranged a few of his action figures at my feet and started to play, waiting for me, sooner or later, to get involved. So I gave up on sleeping, and said: Grandpa is going to work for a bit while you play. He didn't reply, pretending to be absorbed by what he was doing so as to hide his disappointment.

I moved to the living room with pencils, markers, my sketchbook, computer, everything I'd brought down. I wanted to gather ideas, read over the passages of James's story that I intended to work on. But that reading made me think back, I don't know why, to the man in the café, and I looked in my notepad for the sketch I'd done. If it was true that the barista had once known how to draw but that his ability had passed like a fever, then the person I'd portrayed was what remained of a possibility. Which was why, maybe, he'd made an impression on me; I'd glimpsed, beside him, for a few seconds, a white figure I'd sketched from the side, while I'd given him, with the decisive strokes of a marker, a crooked, lined face, stumpy hands. I tried to redo the drawing on a bigger sheet of paper. The man in the bar was life in its definitive form, in its duration, while the indistinct white figure—that one, yes, that was a ghost. But I'd been wrong to draw one next to the other. Once, perhaps, they'd been quite close, but little by little the force of things had caused everything to clot around the man at the bar, and the separation had become irreparable. And I—it occurred to me—what had I come from, what had I separated from? And the question was already inspiring images, when Mario's voice reached me:

—What are you doing, Grandpa? Come here, Dad's back.

Saverio stepped in, still wearing his raincoat, saying to his son: Let's not bother Grandpa. He had a morose look on his face and he muttered that Betta was still at the university, pronouncing the word university as if it was not where they worked but a pub where my daughter drank, snorted drugs, and sang in a throaty voice wearing skintight clothes. I didn't comment, and he informed me that he was going to lock himself in his study to put the final touches—that was the term he used—on his presentation. Mario didn't follow him. He waited on the threshold of the living room, saying nothing. Far from not bothering Grandpa. I sighed, picked myself up, and said: OK, let's go see your toys.

He cheered up considerably. He wanted to show each of them to me one by one, and there were a lot. He listed the names and roles of various repulsive figures that he loved, and then, without asking if I wanted to play, he introduced me to a world of his imagining, everything already decided, inside of which I had to do exactly what he said. The minute I made a mistake he mildly reproached me: Grandpa, you don't get it, you're a horse, don't you see that you're a horse? If on the other hand I got distracted he got upset, he asked me, his voice serious: Don't you want to play anymore?

I often made a mistake, and I was frequently distracted. I seemed to be fading out from boredom, and without my realizing it my mind slipped back to James's short story, and the drawing of the man in the café. For a few seconds I pictured images that seemed decent to me, and I wanted to sketch them. But Mario was saying, Grandpa, watch out for the bear, as well as other animals that, according to him, were in that very moment attacking me, the horse. Or I was simply getting sleepy, because the visionary energy of the child blunted my own, it depressed me, and I felt my eyelids closing. I came back to myself only thanks to a tug and Mario's voice, stern, calling me.

I hoped to have a restorative break when the child, evidently saddened by my meager participation, said he was going to ask his father if he wanted to play with us. I did nothing to hinder him, and I stretched out on the bed. But he came back almost immediately, and I roused myself from my half-sleep, while he, aggrieved, said that his father had promised to play with him as soon as he had finished his work. You and I can play meanwhile, he suggested, without enthusiasm. I got up on my elbows and asked:

—Got any friends?

—One.

—Just one?

—Yeah, he lives on the first floor.

—Here, in this building?

—Yeah.

—And you never go play with him for awhile?

—Mom doesn't send me down.

—And he doesn't visit you?

—No, they don't send him up.

—He's young?

—He's six.

—So he's a big boy.

—Yes, but they still don't let him come over.

—If you never see each other, what kind of friendship is it?

He explained that the friendship was formed on the balcony. He would lower the bucket down to the first floor and exchange things with his friend, whose name was Attilio.

—What things?

—Toys, candy, fruit juice, everything.

—So, you put your stuff in the bucket for him and he puts in his stuff for you?

—No, I'm the only one who puts stuff in.

—And your friend takes it?

—Yeah.

—So he steals your stuff?

—He doesn't steal it, he borrows.

—Does he return what he takes from you?

—No, Mom goes to get it back.

—Does she get mad?

—Super mad.

I understood that the bucket trafficking had created problems for Betta and some tension between the families. The only one who thought he had a friend on the first floor was Mario.

—Want to see how I lower the bucket? he asked, smooth-talking me.

I looked at the glass door: it was getting dark but you could still see the iron bars, the bucket, the cord.

—No, it's cold. I'm also afraid of the balcony.

The child smiled.

—What are you scared of? You're a grown-up.

—My mother, your great-grandmother, was afraid, too.

—No way.

—Yes way. She was afraid of the void.

—What's the void?

I realized I lacked the patience, also the strength, to explain it to him. I replied carelessly:

—It's not a big deal.

Meanwhile there was no trace of Saverio. I suggested getting one of the books I'd given Mario and reading him a fairy tale. I read four of them and felt drained when Betta returned, thoroughly worn out.

She appeared in the room, finding me and her son stretched out on the cot. I'd just started the fifth fable and Mario was listening attentively.

—Leave Grandpa alone, she said. It's my turn.

We went into the kitchen, where she wanted to know if I had read the list of things that I had to be absolutely mindful of while they were away. I admitted that I hadn't. So she dragged me through the house repeating point by point what she'd already told me the night before. She did the same thing at dinner, driving Saverio crazy. He muttered two or three times, Betta, your father's an intelligent man, he gets it. But after dinner, even though she hadn't finished packing yet, she started up again and this time it was a good thing, because it occurred to her that she hadn't given me the pediatrician's number, or the number of a friend of hers who was ready to help were I hard pressed, or the number of the plumber in case, say, the shower or the toilet flush stopped working.

—You'd told me, I mentioned softly, that I could count on Sally, but she's not coming the day after tomorrow.

She replied harshly:

—What's the problem? She'll leave you everything in the freezer. You're too anxious, Dad.

—It's because work's not going well.

—So don't waste time with Mario. Why did you read him fairy tales? Tell him you have to work and you'll see how he entertains himself. Just do me a favor and don't leave him in front of the television. You need to hide the remote control.

—Okay.

—And don't leave him on the balcony, especially if it's cold. His father lets him play the bucket game but I don't like it: the kid on the first floor steals his toys and I have to fight to get them back.

—Do I have to take him to nursery?

—Yes, it's around the corner. I left the address for you on the sheet of paper and I told his teachers.

—Can I keep him home?

—Do whatever you want. Good night, Dad.

—Good night.

—I'll call every night before dinner to see how it's going. Pick up, okay? Otherwise I'll worry.

She left me the task of putting the child to sleep. I found him in his pajamas, seated on my bed, playing with my cell phone. I took it away from him, somewhat abruptly, and said:

—This is Grandpa's, don't touch it.

—Dad lets me use his.

—You can't use mine.

—Yours isn't fun, there aren't any games on it.

—Well then, there's no need for you to play with it.

I placed the phone up high, on a shelf full of knickknacks that he couldn't get to. Mario's mood darkened and he asked me to read him another fairy tale. I told him I'd already read him four and that he was old enough to fall asleep like Grandpa, without a fairy tale. And so I got into my bed, and he into his. I turned off the light. Saverio shouted: I'm the best and you can't stand that, you do everything you can to put me into humiliating situations with these assholes I'm forced to work with. I didn't catch Betta's reply. I slept soundly all night.

CHAPTER TWO

1.

The first day Mario and I spent almost entirely alone was filled with little moments that heightened my anxiety. I struggled to wake up, and it took a while to realize where I was. When I saw that it was nearly eight o'clock, I panicked. I pulled myself up, still in a stupor, and cast my eyes on the child's bed. He wasn't there. My heart started to pound: Surely Betta and Saverio had already left to get to the airport on time, where was Mario? I found him in the kitchen, leafing though one of the books I'd given him. The table was impeccably set for two. I thought it was Betta's doing, but as soon as he saw me he smiled with contentment and said:

—I put the sugar on my side, Grandpa, since you don't take any.

He'd gotten up early, he'd let me sleep, he'd eaten a handful of biscuits, he'd set the table.

—But, he said, I waited for you to turn on the gas.

—Good boy. Tomorrow, remember to wake me up.

—I called you but you didn't answer.

—I was tired, it won't happen again.

—Did you get tired from carrying me?

—Yes.

I prepared his milk, my tea. He drank his milk greedily and ate several more chocolate biscuits. He asked:

—Am I not going to nursery?

—Do you want to go?

—No.

—Don't go then.

He made dramatic signs of satisfaction, then settled down and asked cautiously:

—Are we going to play later?

—I need to work.

—Always?

—Always.

It took forever in the bathroom. He brushed his teeth and washed his face standing on a stool, but then he wet his undershirt and told me where to find another one. By the time I'd forced him to get completely dressed, he said something mysteriously allusive: I have to go. He returned to the bathroom, arranged the stool in front of the toilet, ran to get my book of fairy tales, put it on the stool, pulled down his pants, and sat on the toilet.

—Close the door, Grandpa, he said without lifting his eyes from the book, which he'd opened as if it were on a lectern.

I closed it and went to the living room where all my supplies were. Only a few minutes passed when I heard him call out:

—Grandpa, I did it.

I had to undress and wash him all over again. When it was time once more to get dressed, he naturally wanted to do it himself, but with an unbearable lack of speed, and under my watch.

Sally arrived and I sighed in relief. She appeared in the house with the look of an elegant lady who, despite her heavy body, knows how to dress with style. But she immediately locked herself up in the storage room at the end of the hallway and emerged looking baggy in a ratty T-shirt, shapeless pants, and slippers.

—I leave the child to you, I need to work, I said.

This time she was in a good mood, and she decided to be kind.

—Of course, go ahead, don't worry, little Mario's a good boy. Aren't you a good little boy, Mario?

Mario asked me:

—Grandpa, can I see how you draw?

—No.

—I'll sit next to you, I won't bother you, I'll draw, too.

—Grandpa isn't playing, I said; Grandpa's working.

I shut myself up in the living room. But after only a few minutes I realized that I didn't want to continue working on Henry James. I sank into a chair. I'd slept a great deal, contrary to my habits, and yet I was wiped out, with no desire to dedicate myself to what I'd done, all my life, with pleasure. Rather, it surprised me to think of my body—my body now—lacking the abilities that had given my life meaning. A yen for lucid self-denigration mounted bit by bit. All at once I saw an old man without qualities, of feeble strength, hesitant step, clouded sight, sudden sweats and chills, increasing listlessness interrupted only by weak efforts of will, forced enthusiasm, sincere melancholy. And that image seemed to be my true image, true not only now, in Naples in the house of my adolescence, but—the wave of depression was spreading—true also in Milan for some time, ten years, fifteen, though perhaps less precise than in that moment. Until then I'd managed to lie to myself about being at the peak of my productivity. The artistic life had had its quiet mean, without visible peaks and therefore without sudden valleys. Success, when it had come, had seemed natural to me. I'd never done anything to obtain it or hang onto it: My work was simply deserving. Maybe this was the reason I still thought success was a long-lasting substance that would never deteriorate. As a result it had been easy to neglect the fact that my work was declining, that I was invited less and less frequently to important festivals, that the entire world within which I'd enjoyed a little prestige had been replaced by other worlds I didn't even hear about, by other powerful groups who didn't know who I was, by youthful and aggressive factions who had no idea about my work and who, if they sought me out, did so in order to learn if I could be of some use in launching their careers. Here though—I said to myself—are signs of decline I can't ignore anymore, as violent as dreams that crack glass: the offensive call from my publisher; the worn-out imagination I couldn't manage to revive; and my daughter, my only daughter, who'd ensnared me, unawares, in the role of the elderly grandfather.

I sighed heavily, aware that I was making an instinctive gesture with my hand, like Mario. And I was almost happy that Sally was calling me. Grandpa, she was saying aloud in a sugar-coated way, Grandpa. Apparently, since she didn't know what name to give me, she addressed me using the same term as the child, believing she was doing the right thing. Or maybe, given that I was Mario's grandfather, she thought of me as the grandfather of all grandfathers, anyone's grandfather, even her grandfather, even though, god help me, she was hardly a young woman. She said loudly, knocking at the door and opening it right away:

—Grandpa, excuse me, little Mario has turned on the television and he doesn't want to turn it off.

—What television?

—The television. Didn't Miss Betta tell you he isn't supposed to watch it?

—Yes.

—Well, Grandpa, do something.

—Don't call me Grandpa. I'm not your grandpa and I don't feel like Mario's grandpa, either.

I got out of the chair with a groan and followed her into the hallway. The television was like a roaring airplane interrupted by blaring, virile voices.

—Where is the child?

—In Mr. Saverio's study.

—Sally, if Mario does something he shouldn't be doing, all you need to do is tell him not to, without calling me.

—But he doesn't listen to me. And I can't slap him, you can.

—A four-year-old child shouldn't be slapped.

—Well, then, a *tottò* on the hands.

—I don't know what a *tottò* is.

Actually I knew what it meant, but the sound repulsed me. I belonged to the generation that had started talking to children in the Italian of adults.

—Miss Betta says *tottò*.

—So she can give him a *tottò* on his little hands when she gets back.

I followed her into Saverio's study, which reeked of garlic and detergent. Little Mario was sitting in front of the TV, and he turned around abruptly. The woman said:

—See that I really did call him?

—You shouldn't tell on people, the child said.

—You should if it's necessary, I said, intervening. In any case, the volume is so high I can't work. Turn it off.

—Then I'll turn it down, the child said, grabbing the remote control.

I took it out of his hands and switched off the screen. After which I explained to him, calmly:

—Mario, for all I care, you can watch television for as long as you like, morning, afternoon, and evening. But your mother doesn't want you to, and if she doesn't want you to then Sally and I don't want you to, either. Therefore when Sally tells you to turn it off, you turn it off. And if I tell you to turn it off, don't you ever try to tell me: Then I'll turn it down. Got that?

The child looked down at the floor and nodded. Then he looked up at the remote control that I was holding, as if he wanted to take it from me.

—Can I show you how to open it and see the batteries?

—No, you aren't to touch this anymore.

—Then what do I do?

—Why don't you go play?

—On the balcony?

—No.

—It's sunny.

—I said no.

—Then can I come see how you draw?

He was stubborn, he didn't give in. I stared him down for a while, mainly to convey my aversion. When I realized that his upper lip was sweaty I quickly let up.

—Fine, but don't bother me.

—I won't bother you.

—Don't say: Grandpa, I want this, let's do this.

—I won't.

—You have to stay put, quietly.

—Okay. But first I'm going to pee.

He ran away, I heard him locking the bathroom door. Sally, who had stood there silently the whole time, took advantage to reproach me:

—A grandfather shouldn't talk that way.

—What do you mean?

—You've terrified him, poor kid.

—You're the one who wanted me to slap him.

—A slap makes sense, not this.

—This what?

—This nasty tone of yours. If you're so busy and cranky, I'll take the child.

It hadn't occurred to me that I'd used any tone in particular. Maybe she was the one I needed to be more severe with. Mario came back hurriedly. His eyes were red, as if he'd rubbed them hard.

—I'm ready.

Making an effort to sound playful, I asked:

—Would you rather see how I work, or how Sally works?

He turned from me to Sally pretending to look hesitant, then, coming back to me, shouted with excessive glee:

—How you work.

And off he went to the living room with lively steps. I said to Sally: As you can see, he prefers me. She didn't look convinced, and replied that she was going to start cooking. I watched her as she left Saverio's study. She was a little curvy, something that made her look even smaller in stature. In a flash I recalled that she wouldn't be coming the next day: a whole day of me alone with the child. I suggested to her quickly, don't take a day off, I'll pay you myself for the entire day: Come at nine in the morning, leave at eight, you don't need to clean the house, all you need to do is watch little Mario. She didn't even turn around. She replied: I'm busy tomorrow, it's an important day, my future gets decided. Old sourpuss. The future, always the future, what future did she have in store? I went back to the living room.

2.

Mario was moving a chair as close as possible to mine.

—Can I use your computer? he asked.

—Don't even think about it.

I hesitated before sitting down. I was tempted to pick up the cell phone and yell at the publisher: I don't give a fuck about oxygen, about brightness, tell me in plain words what's wrong with it, because otherwise I'll quit the job and forsake the pittance you'll give me for it, I don't want to waste time.

But I didn't do it, and the anguish of old age poked its head up once more. I needed that work, and not for money—my house in Milan and my savings kept me comfortably—but because I was scared to think of myself free from the obligations of work. For at least fifty years I'd moved from one deadline to the next, always under the gun, and the anxiety of failing to suitably tackle one then another, followed by the pleasure of successfully doing just that, was a seesaw without which—I finally confessed to myself outright—I couldn't bear to picture myself. No, no, better to still keep saying for a while, to acquaintances, to my family, to my son-in-law, above all to myself: I need to work on James, I'm extremely behind, I have to come up with something as soon as possible. Thus, under Mario's attentive gaze, I resumed examining my sketches, especially the chaotic ones from two nights back.

At first I only did it to calm down. I looked at the pages, I appreciated the good smell of cooking that was entering the room in spite of the closed door, and now and then out of the corner of my eye I kept watch on the boy, who was keeping his word, never scraping his chair, scarcely breathing. The whole time Mario stared at the pages with me, as if we were having a contest to see who would get tired first. But then at a certain point I stopped being aware of him. I got an idea: to use the drawings of the apartment the way it had been many years ago as a backdrop for the New York house in James's story. The hypothesis stirred me, here was a good way to begin: I'd make rooms on the other side of the ocean, from the 1800s, collide with rooms in a house in Naples, from the mid twentieth century. Great. With my pencil I immediately began to isolate, among the disorder of those crammed, marked-up pages, certain details that seemed useful to me. And my mind fired up so quickly that when Mario called me, feebly—it was a moment in which everything was coming together, I could picture it all vividly—I told him sharply: Be quiet, you promised. But he repeated, softy:

—Grandpa.

—What was our deal?

—I have to be quiet and not move.

—Exactly.

—But I just have to tell you *one* thing.

—Just one. What is it?

He pointed to a few strokes of the black marker, in a corner on the right side of the page that I was looking over. He said:

—That's you.

I looked at the drawing, it was an absentminded scribble. Perhaps it represented a young man gripping a knife, maybe a boy with a candle, but in such a vague way, as if my hand had strayed without meaning to into that corner. When had I done it? The other night? A little while ago? The lines writhed swiftly, a flicker that barely presented itself before disappearing. I didn't dislike it, it reminded me of the stuff I knew how to do when I was a boy, and it moved me that, contrary to my beliefs, I'd captured something from those years—something of what I was able to draw when I lived in that apartment with my parents and my brothers. I'll use it, I told myself, it's good. And I asked the boy:

—Do you like it?

—I guess. It sort of scares me.

—It's not me, it's a doodle.

—It's you, Grandpa, I'll show you.

He slipped down from the chair with a resolute look.

—Where are you going?

—To get the photo album, come, bring the drawing.

He waited for me to get up, taking me by the hand as if we might lose one another. When I opened the living room door, we were assaulted by a cold blast. Evidently Sally, to air things out, to dry the wet floors, had opened every window, and now the apartment was freezing. On top of that, the noise of the traffic, without the protection of the double-paned glass, rose up harshly. We went into my daughter's study; there, too, the window was wide open, and the racket from outside was suffocating shouts from afar, like someone pounding a rug with a carpet beater. Mario dragged a chair up to a cabinet full of doors. I tried to stop him.

—Tell me where the album is and I'll get it for you, I told him, but in vain. He relished climbing. He opened one of the doors, turning the key. He pried out an old-fashioned album, dark green, and handed it to me.

—You have to close it up, I reminded him.

He closed it.

—And lock.

Ably he turned the key.

—You're a dwarf, I told him.

—No, I'm not.

—Yes, that's exactly what you are, a dwarf.

—It's not true, I'm a little boy, he said, getting upset.

—All right, sorry, you're a little boy, Grandpa's stupid and says stupid things, stupidly. Never mind.

I helped him jump off the chair—but this time he tried to free his hand, he wanted to jump on his own, something I tried to prevent—and when he landed with a little yelp of joy, he asked me:

—Did you mean I'm one of the seven dwarves?

—Yes, I replied. And I explained that he'd been wrong to get offended, it was a compliment, it meant: You're sensible and wise. Then I set the album on the desk and asked him where the picture he wanted to show me was. I knew the album well: It contained family photographs that had been passed down from my mother to my wife and, when my wife died, to Betta. The child leafed through it with expertise and showed me an image in which I was with my mother and my brothers. I had no memory of it, I must have always looked at it unwillingly. I'd considered every moment of my adolescence a hateful constriction. Surely my father had taken the picture, he looked at us through the camera and we looked at him. Everyone but me was smiling. How old was I? Twelve, thirteen? My face was repugnant: long, thin, unrefined. Time had left every millimeter of the picture intact, apart from my own contours. Or maybe the image had always been like this, and some fault in the developing had damaged only my outline.

Nothing about the face and stringy body appeared complete. I had no mouth, no nose, my eyes were hidden by the thick arcing shadow of my brows, my hair dissolved in the albumen of the sky. Of that instant frozen by the camera, I only recognized the flash of hatred for my father. I looked at him without eyes, with aversion, because of his gambling habit, how he'd raised us in poverty, the fury he'd embodied and unleashed onto my mother, onto us, when he didn't have a hand to play. The aversion had been rendered precisely, and now it repulsed me.

—See how it's you? Mario said.

—Not really.

He brought my drawing alongside the photograph.

—Don't lie, Grandpa. It's you.

—I wasn't like that, it's the picture that makes me look that way.

—But that's exactly how you drew yourself, look. You're really ugly.

I shuddered:

—Yes, indeed, but it's a bit mean of you to say so.

—Dad says you're always supposed to tell the truth.

I guessed it was Saverio who had called me ugly, in that picture and perhaps in general. Bodies—these tattered shreds of nature—need affinity to get along, and my son-in-law and I had never managed to feel affinity for one another. I still heard the screams, the carpet pounding was getting louder. I examined the facade of the building across the street, where no one was screaming or beating a carpet. I asked:

—Grandpa, in addition to being ugly, is also a bit deaf. Do you hear that shouting?

Closing the album, he replied:

—Yes, it's Sally.

—Sally? Why didn't you say so?

—I didn't want to bother you.

I pulled on my earlobe, the lobe of my right ear, hoping to improve my hearing. The shouts were coming from the room where we slept. I went to see what was happening, and Mario trailed me as if he already knew. Sally was on the balcony, the glass door was closed. She was banging her hands against the double-paned glass but the blows and her shouts—Grandpa, little Mario!—resounded weakly in the room and throughout the apartment, precisely because of the double-paned glass. I remembered Betta's warnings: The balcony door didn't work well. I thought to myself, annoyed: The publisher, Mario, Sally, it's impossible to concentrate. The woman should have been dealing with me and the child, instead here I was wasting my time because she was scatterbrained. She'd opened every window in the house and then gone onto the balcony without thinking that the wind would have slammed the door shut. And now there she was, shouting for help.

—Stop banging on the glass, I said. We're here.

—I've been calling out for half an hour.

—Oh, come on.

—Can't you hear?

—I'm a bit deaf.

—You know how to open up?

—No.

—Mister Saverio didn't teach you?

—No.

Sally looked dejected and pounded the glass yet again. I felt we had, in that moment, twinned feelings: Both of us exasperated by the time we were wasting, each blaming the other, and this made me feel unexpectedly close to her. Mario on the other hand was getting on my nerves, he wanted to play at every occasion.

—Grandpa, I know how to open it.

I didn't answer him. I asked Sally:

—Can't you open it from outside?

—If I could I wouldn't be calling you. There's no handle outside.

—What do you mean there's no handle?

—What do I know, Mister Saverio bought it this way. But to release it from inside all you have to do is pull up, hard, then pull down.

Mario stepped in:

—Get it, Grandpa? You pull this way, then turn that way.

He motioned precisely with his hands, and I repeated after him without even realizing.

—Like that, he said approvingly. Should I get a chair and help you?

—I'll do it myself.

I set to it but without success. The door wouldn't open.

—You have to do it hard, as hard as Dad.

—Dad's young, I'm old.

I tried again. I pushed the handle up and then down, with tremendous resolution. Still nothing.

—I can't stand here all day, Sally said, starting to fret. I have other houses to get to. Call the fire department.

—What the hell are you talking about?

The child tugged on me, but I ignored him. Then, to attract my attention, he started repeatedly striking my leg with a closed fist.

—I have an idea.

—Keep it to yourself and let me think.

He kept punching my leg. I grunted:

—Speak.

—Sally lowers the bucket and pulls up the empty space. When it's all gone she climbs over and leaves.

Sally, exasperated, screamed:

—If I don't get to work they'll fire me. Please do something. When the door doesn't open you need a screwdriver.

—Yes, Mario confirmed. Dad opens it with a screwdriver, sometimes. I can help you, should I go get the screwdriver?

—You'll be of more help if you stop talking.

I was frazzled, I couldn't concentrate. How long had it been since I'd used a screwdriver, pliers, a wrench? I kept thinking about the scant strokes I'd made at the edge of the page and, at the same time, Mario's voice, insistent, that drew attention to—rather, that pointed out to me—similarities between those strokes and the teenager in the photo. I was at risk at that age, I did poorly at school, I struggled with Latin. My father had sent me to a small foundry close to our house, a place that no longer existed. For a few months my hand and my mind found new direction, and perhaps the scrawls I'd made had something to do with that period. I need to make sketches like that, I told myself, and I felt that I was ready, my mind wouldn't let up, it pinned me to my surroundings, rapidly suggesting ideas, not for freeing Sally but for drawing after drawing; I saw them emerge, disappear. I pictured a doodled version of myself as a boy, one who knew how to turn the door handle the right way, and could capably use a screwdriver. I felt I could access that efficient figure without lifting pencil from paper, moving instead directly from the tips of my already gnarled, grease-stained hands, then rising up again through my strong arms and tense neck, until it reached the ugly grin on my face. I had so many versions of those teenagers in mind. That throng was mutations of me between the ages of twelve and twenty, when I stopped growing and found the strength to escape that house. Now I wanted to try a backflip, over more than fifty years of adult work, down down down to the first time I took a stab at creating images. It was almost as if it were really possible to put today's passionate, red-hot working and reworking behind me and sink into an absolute zero, into a hole in the ice where everything was preserved. I seized the handle, and with rage—rage, not ire—I pushed it, first up, then down. I felt a click, pulled the door, and the door opened.

—About time, Sally sputtered, and returned indoors nearly shouting: I'm out of here, I'm late.

She explained what to do for lunch and for dinner that day and the next, but all the while she spoke only to Mario; I no longer inspired any trust in her. She shut herself in the storeroom, came out looking like an elegant elderly woman, and then off she went.

I sat down on the edge of my bed. Mario quickly removed his shoes, climbed up, and started to jump off of it with squeals of joy, undoing Sally's work. He asked: Are you going to jump too, Grandpa? The glass door was still wide open, the balcony surged out against a deep-blue sky. I saw a yellowish weed sprouting up from the black, uneven traces of soil between the tiles. I said to the boy:

—You can't pull up empty space with a bucket, Mario. Don't you dare play that game you were talking about. The empty space is always there, and if you go over the railing and jump, you die. Didn't Dad tell you that? All he told you was that I was incredibly ugly?

Then I, too, took off my shoes, I got up on the bed, and we jumped for a while, holding hands. I felt my heart in my chest like a huge ball of live flesh that went up and down from my stomach to my throat and back again.

3.

Mario must have thought that the time for high jinks had now begun. Actually I'd simply meant to throw him a bone and then get back to work. We ate Sally's food, which was delicious, and already, as we ate, I tried to capture one of the images that had come to me. I brought a morsel to my mouth with one hand and I quickly sketched small dense figures with the other, though I had to admit they weren't turning out very well. The child's fault: He never quit, he suggested, endlessly, that we play games after lunch that were, according to him, incredibly entertaining. In the end I gave in. Let's clean up and then we'll do something fun, but just for a while, you know that Grandpa's busy.

I cleaned up as per his instructions, and he reproached me all the while. Everything had to go back to its proper place and it was useless telling him that Sally would have dealt with it later. At first I thought it was his sense of obedience to his parents that made him so scrupulous, but that wasn't it. He adored being praised, and since Mother and Father surely faked enthusiasm for the disciplined way he handled any given object, he expected I'd do the same thing. When I said: Who cares where the salt shaker goes, leave it there, don't be annoying, he tightened his lips and looked at me, disoriented. I could only curb his pedantry by telling him that the longer we spent putting every last thing in its place, the less time we'd have to play. So he hastily accepted a perfunctory straightening-up and asked: Can we start?

I was forced into playing both ladder and horse. The first made me yawn, constantly. It consisted of pulling the stepladder out of the closet, opening it and making sure it was sturdy, climbing to the top, and then climbing down again. At first he proceeded rung by rung and I held him from behind so that he wouldn't fall, something that drove him crazy since, in his opinion, there was no reason for me to spot him. Then, by means of cautious but continuous protests, he convinced me to let him climb while I stayed at the bottom of the ladder and held him by the arm. In the end he rebelled outright:

—I know how to climb by myself, don't hold me.

—And if you fall?

—I won't.

—But if you do, I'll leave you to cry on the floor.

—Okay.

—And let this be clear: You climb three times, that's it.

—No, thirty.

—How much is thirty, in your opinion?

—A lot.

Seeing him go up and down, tirelessly, wore me out. I dragged a chair over to the ladder and sat down, but I forced myself to monitor any tiny faltering in his movements so that I could leap up in time. It was amazing, the amount of energy in that little body. What took place on his skin, under his skin, in his flesh, in his bones, in his blood? Breath, nutrition. Oxygen, water, electromagnetic storms, protein, waste. How he tightened his lips. And the way he looked up, the effort those too-short legs had to make in order to span the gaps between the rungs with ease, hands tight on the metal beams. Not to mention the descent, at once timid and bold, one foot placed on the rung below while the other was already slowly sliding off, losing its grip. Little determined being, now looking up, now down, the fear and joy of risk. I only got him to stop by agreeing that we would immediately proceed to the second game.

So we moved on to playing horse. Moaning and groaning, I had to get on all fours. He climbed up and straddled me and, holding me by the sweater, proceeded to command with authority: giddyup, trot, gallop. If I was too slow in obeying he dealt me blows to the ribs with his heels, shouting: I said gallop, are you deaf? I was deaf, indeed, and tired, and in bad shape, to a degree he couldn't possibly imagine. He was a crass little thing, despite his impressive vocabulary. He started to really think I was a horse, and in fact he stopped calling me Grandpa, now he called me Furia, a name Saverio had passed on to him. But the fury was in him, his whole being possessed by an uncontrolled energy, a pure expansion of vitality enclosing my inadequate body like a cyst, every move injuring my wrists, my knees, my ribs. Nevertheless I strove at least to go around the house, down the hall, into the kitchen, Betta's study, living room, foyer, Saverio's alcove, and finally back to our room, where the balcony was still open and it was very cold. By this point I was boiling hot: Blood flowed from the farther reaches of my body like lava enflaming my veins and heart. I was dripping with sweat, more sweat than I sometimes produced at night. If, in Mario's body, the secret workings of physics and chemistry were joyfully violent, in mine they were sad, painfully melancholy, their equations and reactions increasingly abused, increasingly unsolved, like the classwork of unwilling students. I seized the child with one arm and pulled him down from the croup before he could say: Again.

—The horse is tired, I said, wheezing.

—No.

—He is, he's exhausted.

I put him on the floor and I stretched out beside him on the icy tiles.

—Let's catch our breath now.

—I don't need to catch my breath, Grandpa. Let's do it again.

—Don't even think of it.

—Dad does five.

—I do one, that's what you get.

—Please.

—I have to work.

—What about me?

—You have your action figures, stay here and play with all of them.

—Can I bring my toys into the room with you?

—No, you'll distract me.

—You're mean.

—Yes, very mean.

—I'll tell Mom.

—Your mom already knows.

—Then I'll tell Dad.

—Tell anyone you want.

—My dad'll punch you.

—If I say boo to your father he'll poop in his pants.

—Say it again.

—Boo.

—No, the other thing.

—He'll poop in his pants.

He laughed.

—Again.

—He'll poop in his pants.

He laughed hysterically for a long time. I sat up, first on the floor, then I leaned against the edge of the bed and pulled myself up. The sweat had congealed on my back and chest and now I felt cold. I went to shut the balcony door.

—Again, Grandpa, Mario asked, looking up at me.

—What?

—He poops in his pants.

—No dirty words.

—You said it.

—I said he poops in his pants?

He immediately started laughing again, shouting out:

—Yes, yes yes.

Even the delighted violence that gurgled from that wide-open mouth, exposing its tiny teeth, disturbed me. I envied the reckless hilarity on his face and in his throat. I didn't know if I'd ever laughed like that, certainly I had no memory of it. There was such force in the way he laughed at what was at once vapid and essential. He was laughing at trivial words used to describe his father's body, and it was a laughter—I thought—unclouded by anguish. I wandered around the room. I glanced, distracted, at his drawings on the walls, all stick figures and green grass and indecipherable scrawls.

—Do you like them? he asked.

—They're too light, I said. And I proceeded to knock all the action figures that Sally had carefully arranged on the shelves onto the floor. After that I lifted up a big box chock-ablock with toys and let them pour out, leaving him speechless. The objects fell all around him, striking the floor as if they were dancing. I waved goodbye with my hand and said:

—Have fun.

He stared at me, stunned, red in the face.

—I don't have fun on my own, he said, vexed.

—I do. And you better not bother me, otherwise there'll be trouble.

4.

I had no fun at all. Playing with the child had not only worn me out but depleted energy from the drawings I'd felt the urgency to pin down. Glimpsing them had rendered them accessible, and they had thus lost the allure of being unrepresentable. Now they sat there like ailing beasts waiting, mutely and blindly, either to heal or die. And so the prospect of hunting them down, trying to dredge them up from nothing with the swift line that had arrived for the drawing Mario had spotted, turned increasingly sluggish. All I did was make irritated marks, wishing my hand would obey me again.

I thought imagination had veiled eyes. My old body, by now, was too distant from the aborted adolescents that flashed for a second and then broke apart, grumbling inside me with a deafening boom. And yet they were the ones—I thought—the ghosts that might be useful to me. Hostile, dangerous. That unconscious scribble I'd made in one corner of the page was their vanguard. He actually gripped a knife, and along with the knife the yearning to use it, driving it into the body of a rude passerby, into my father's throat, between Mena's hard breasts when she'd left me, into the chest of the handsome young guy who'd taken her away. Between the ages of twelve and sixteen I'd always been looking for an opportunity, I wanted to find an egress for the bloodthirstiness that made my head hurt. If I'd used that knife even once, if I'd done so only as a threat, I'd have become more suited to the streets: the Lavinaio, the Carmine, the Duchessa. It wasn't a matter of fantasies triggered by hormonal ups and downs. My fantasies back then were something different, they were about becoming an artist, even though no one in my house knew what that meant, not my father or my grandfather, not one of my ancestors. It was realistic, on the other hand, become cocky, screw up, get thrown in jail, and feel in my hands the ability to kill, kill like a camorrista, do it according to a design that was entirely in keeping with the streets through which I moved until late at night, streets of illicit trafficking, whores, ruffians. A far cry from pencils, crayons, watercolors, paints. That feeble part of me didn't belong there. During adolescence I'd had hands ready for something quite different. When my father sent me to the foundry he wasn't being wicked, poor man, he was giving both himself and me a lesson in realism. The tradition in my extremely sprawling family tree was to be a mechanic. Or an electrician, like my father. Or a turner like my grandfather. This was what was probable, and also what was possible. Putting together, taking apart, screwing, unscrewing, nails always black, fingertips thick, palms wide and hard. Or slaving away unloading at the docks, or at the fruit and vegetable market. Or being a gofer in a workshop, or a waiter, or starting up a little shop, getting a job for life working for the railroad. Or living by my wits, by hustling, by the wiles of necessity, leaving no doubt that I only ever have women on my mind, that I'm never satisfied with any of them, that I collect them, caress them, take advantage of them, beating them if they don't want to bend over nice and quiet, oh I wanted it, some of the guys I played with had done all that, always in keeping with the city neighborhood we'd been raised in. Or to reject the dark chasms of women and slip into male bodies with the excuse of humiliating them, or only because it's easier to feel at home with known actions and reactions, or because the drives are confused, the flesh is uncertain, always moving without resolution from men to women, from women to men, holes here and holes there, so many useless distinctions. I'd made efforts, in those years, to escape the numerous possible violent paths of my surroundings, all of them already embedded in the obscenity of the dialect I'd known since I was a child: I'll rip your guts out, I'll fuck you up the ass, I'll crack your ass open. It was as if various human types were lurking in my body, some violent, others wretched. For example, there were those attuned to the rule of minding their own fucking business. When they rose up, I got a devil-may-care smirk on my face, a look of arrogant acquiescence. I had a disposition for that, too: Be quiet so as not to collide, not offend, talk only to agree, to convey kindness, praise, be everyone's friend, absolutely everyone's, which ends up meaning nobody's, and so to appear innocuous, and thus someone to spend time with, and meanwhile to amass spite for everyone, and harm in secret. I was a crowd of variations. Then, right, by pure chance, I'd started with pencils, with paints, only by chance, and I'd derived a surprising pleasure from it. From that point ensued the long battle to crush all my other spirits and to banish them to the farthest reaches of my blood. I didn't allow them to take another drink. And it took such grit to fend off the underlying truth of their cutting murmurs: What do you want, asshole, you talk so fine, think you're better than us, you piece of shit? You're nothing, you motherfucker, you're the brush that scrubs my toilet. The slightest uncertainty would have sufficed: failure at school, even a nasty comment about my first art show, a pan that breaks the heart, and I'd have capitulated. Insecurity would have seeped through that crack, and desperation, and unhappiness, and it would have annihilated the little man I longed to become: the kind that used sophisticated words, had subtle feelings, a sense of responsibility, a sage defense of the good, standard sexuality, life absorbed by a single great passion: to produce work in an endless cycle, big work, small work, medium work, nothing interested me more. But I'd done it, I'd managed, always gasping for breath, to plug up the cracks one by one. And I'd become flesh, the rest were ghosts. But now here they were, they were parked in the living room of the apartment in which I'd grown up, the apartment transformed today into Betta's home, and Saverio's and Mario's. They'd gathered there with their dialect, with their uncouth desires and ways, their nastiness always ready to explode over the tiniest conflict. They didn't forgive me for having chosen the least likely variation and for having defended it, having stood up to them without ceding an inch. I'd chased them away, but never completely. Only my death would have crushed them definitively, erasing the body they always aspired to, and, like it or not, that kept them alive. As weak as they were they never stopped turning up, especially the boy with the knife, whom I drove away, however, with a stroke of my hand, eyes closed, like a refined person. That stroke was the fruit of highly disciplined training. I'd learned to blur every sentiment, reduce my reactions to almost nothing, feel neither love nor pain, pass off for compassion what was merely the absence of any carnal, palpitating affectivity. By the time I rummaged through Ada's notebooks, she'd been dead for years. She wrote that it had been my fault, she'd turned to infidelity to prove to herself that she existed apart from me. For a long time I dreamed with eyes open that she was still alive, and that I was slitting her throat. But I stood up to that dream every time with a polite gesture of refusal, and in the end I blunted her, I thought I understood her reasons, I ceased to dream, instead I started to love her ghost the way I'd loved her living body. Maybe—I thought—I can illustrate James with these ghosts. Now let me go see what the kid's doing, goddamn pain in the ass.

I came back to the concrete dimensions of the living room by sheer force of will. The afternoon light was fading. And I was about to get up from the chair when the doorbell began ringing energetically. One of my legs had fallen asleep; it tingled in a bothersome way, I barely felt my shoe touching the floor. Another ring, heartier than the first. I shouted:

—Mario, are you capable of opening the door? Oh Mario, please?

The only reply was a third, long, furious pressing of the bell. I limped across the living room and the foyer, I opened the door, and I found myself in front of a huge woman with black hair, a dye job that tended toward midnight blue, and small eyes on a wide face. She was anxious and quite pale. She'd left the elevator door open and held Mario, inexplicably, by the hand.

I had a prolonged moment of disorientation. What was the child doing outside the house, on the landing, with that stranger? And the woman also seemed disoriented, she didn't expect that an elderly unknown man would have opened up, his hair in disarray, one of his shirttails sticking out of his pants. There was a confused back and forth: I asked Mario, gruffly, what he was doing outside the house; the woman asked me, harshly, if Signora Cajuri was in, that is to say, Betta. I responded no, she's not, but who are you? The woman raised her voice, saying why don't you tell me who you are, sir? I somewhat stupidly replied, I'm the grandfather of this child, the father of Signora Cajuri. And so on, until the situation grew clearer and settled into the Neapolitan cadences of my childhood.

—Sir, were you the one who sent this kid down to me with his toys?

—No.

—Then who was it?

—He did it on his own.

—On his own? And you didn't realize that he left this apartment, went down five flights, and knocked on my door?

—No.

—No, eh? You're no different than your daughter, when she's busy being a professor she tells her son, go on, bring your toys down to the boy on the first floor and play; but then she gets pissed if the little gentleman learns a few bad words?

—Ma'am, I assure you that I'd never have sent the child down to you, I got distracted, I'm sorry.

—Distracted or not, if the kid had fallen on the stairs and broken his head your daughter's the type to blame my son.

—I'm sorry, it won't happen again.

—Another thing that shouldn't happen is when your maid throws dirty water off the balcony so it ruins the clothes I've put out to dry, something she does practically every other day.

—I'll mention it to Betta, she'll take care of it.

—Thanks, and you can also tell her that she'd better stop saying that my son steals his toys. If my son steals toys, then we'd better keep our sons and our toys to ourselves. Because it's not like the lady's the professor and I'm the free babysitter. I have four kids and a house to run and I don't have time to waste. So this is what I have to say. If the kid keeps sending down the bucket I'll cut the cord and throw the thing away.

—Just as well. But where are the toys Mario took down?

—So you think my son stole them, too?

—No, I didn't say stealing, they're kids. I just wanted to know.

—Okay, if it's just to know, let's do this: When my husband gets home I'll send him up to bring you the toys, and that way you can tell him to his face that our son steals. Go on, Mario, go to your grandfather: You're a family full of shit, from the first generation to the last. Have a nice evening.

She shoved the child toward me, rudely, and slipped into the elevator, banging the iron door behind her, and vanished with a shuddering of the cage.

I pulled Mario inside and closed the door. The child, hostile, said:

—I want my toys, I need them.

I kneeled down and seized him by the arms:

—How dare you leave the house? If I tell you to stay in your room, you have to stay in your room. From this moment, this moment, Mario—look at me—you either do what I say or I lock you up in the closet.

The child didn't look down, he wriggled away, he kicked and said:

—You better watch out or I'll lock you up in the closet.

He pronounced this threatening retort with an effort that wore him out, and the next instant he burst into tears.

I regretted making him cry, and I quickly backpedaled. I tried to console him, I said: Enough, now I'll cry, too. I said: I'm going into the closet to lock myself in. It was useless. At first he cried for real, then he drew it out, mechanically, and he went on like this for about twenty minutes, sniffling, pushing me away when I tried to help him blow his nose. Now and then, between sobs, he kept saying: I'm telling Dad when he gets back.

5.

Even though I let him turn on the gas to heat up the dinner Sally had made, even though I let him handle an extremely sharp knife which he'd arbitrarily appropriated while setting the table, things between us didn't improve.

—Keep the knife, but I'm cutting up the meat.

—No, I know how.

—I believe you know how, but when Grandpa's here, Grandpa cuts up your meat.

—You're not my grandfather.

—No? Then who's my grandson?

—No one.

If Mario didn't want to make peace with me, I had even less desire to make peace with him, given that the more loving and agreeable we were, the less he left me alone. But I was worried because the time for Betta's call was approaching and I didn't want the child to alarm her, she already had enough problems with the jealous inquisitor she was married to. And so as we washed up the dishes from lunch and dinner—he, albeit sulky, continued to think of himself as my helper, procuring soap, sponge, dishcloth, everything I needed, throwing himself into it as if it were a matter of life or death—I started spritzing him with a little water, saying each time: Gotcha. For a while he remained a hostile helper, his head lowered, refusing, resolutely, to budge.

—Gotcha.

—Stop it, Grandpa.

—Gotcha.

—I said stop it.

—Gotcha.

Then he started to pretend to complain, but he struggled to contain a smile.

—You got soap in my eyes.

—Let's see?

—It stings.

—Don't be silly, it's nothing.

Finally he began to look at me askance, to wonder if I

really wanted to play, and when he was convinced, he tried
to spritz me with a little water on his end, saying, Gotcha.
And so, from one gotcha to the next—as a result of horsing
around he lost his balance and was about to fall off the chair
he'd been standing on in order to help me, but thank goodness I grabbed him in time—the tension between us seemed
to slacken. And we went into the living room to watch a little TV.

—What, Grandpa?

—Let's choose.

—Can we watch something animalated?

—Animated.

He struggled to accept that cartoons weren't animals. He
listed geese, goslings, rabbits, mice, shrews, a punctilious cata-
log of the creatures one saw in cartoons, clear proof that cartoons were indeed animals. And right after that he involved me
in a conversation about the meaning of animal, animate, animated, and animation. I said: They're drawings that move,
talk, have a soul. He wanted to know what a soul was. A type
of breath, I replied, that lets us move, run, talk, draw, play
tricks on one another. He stubbornly insisted that animals in
cartoons did precisely all those things. Then little by little he
looked convinced and asked:

—Can cartoons breathe?

—No, the people who draw them give that.

—Your drawings don't move.

—Well, they're not cartoons.

—And why don't you make them animated?

—If they ask me to, I will.

—Maybe they don't let really old people to do it because
they're for little kids.

—They'd let me do it.

—They'd let you because you're famous?

—Do you know what famous means?

—Mom told me: It means people you don't know know who you are.

—That's right, that's what it means.

—I told my teacher you're famous.

—What did she say?

—She asked me your name.

—Did you know?

—I asked Mom and then I told her.

—Let's see if you said it right: Let's hear Grandpa's name.

—Daniele Mallarico.

—Bravo. And what did the teacher say?

—That she'd never heard of you.

I realized that this had disappointed him and I explained that there were various levels of fame, that mine wasn't high enough for the teacher. But as I was speaking it occurred to me that I, too, felt a bit disappointed, and so to prevent our shared disappointment from becoming a bad mood I went back to suggesting that we watch some television. But it was a trial to find the remote control; I'd sequestered it from him and I couldn't remember where I'd put it. I wandered anxiously through the house, tailed by the child. I turned on the lights in each room, I made an effort to look on tables, desks, and shelves without getting distracted—an undertaking that was growing increasingly difficult for me since every time I looked for something I ended up thinking about something else—and when the reconnaissance was finished and I came out of the room, he diligently turned off the lights behind me. We made two or three exploratory rounds, and naturally the one who found the remote control was him, not me: It was in the living room under one of my sketchbooks. He took command of it with enormous enthusiasm, I couldn't pry it away from him. *I* found it, he said, and *I'll* turn on the television. I replied: You just get to turn it on. No, he said, almost shouting, I also get to change the channels. And he was already tightening his lips, his eyes were already hostile. I was about to grab it from him and say: Stop it, either listen to me or go to bed, when the phone rang. Fine, I said, quickly giving in, keep it. And as he followed me, bustling about with the remote control, I went into the kitchen where the cordless phone was.

It was Betta, and she sounded short on time. I heard a din in the background, the sound of silverware, it seemed. Someone called her and she said, with forced cheer: Be right there! Then she said to me:

—Why aren't you picking up your cell phone?

—It's muted.

—Everything OK?

—It's going great.

—Did Mario eat?

—More than I did. How are you?

—Fine.

—Your talk?

—It went fine.

—Things with Saverio?

—He won't let up, he just had a meltdown.

—Tell him to go fuck himself.

—Dad, watch your language.

—Sorry.

—Did Mario hear you?

—No, he's busy dismantling the remote control.

—Put him on and I'll say hi.

—Mario, you want to talk to Mom?

I hoped that Mario would refuse, but instead he dropped the batteries from the remote control on the floor and ran to the telephone. I heard him saying things like: no, yes, come back soon, I love you. But just when the call seemed to have reached its conclusion, he added: I cried. His mother must have said something quite complicated because he listened without answering back. In the end he almost whispered:

Good night, Mom, and kissed the phone ten times, saying, finally, after the kisses: Good night, love you so much, I love Dad, too.

He handed over the phone. I grumbled:

—You didn't have to tell her that you cried.

—That's all I said.

—All? What else was there to say?

—I know what.

—Such as?

—You hurt my arms.

—Come on, I just squeezed you a little.

—You squeezed me hard. Can we watch television?

—Your mother doesn't want you to.

—We won't tell her.

—And yet when it came to telling her you cried, you told her.

—Sorry. I won't tell her about the television.

—If you don't know how to put the batteries back into the remote yourself, don't count on me. I don't know.

He capably reinstalled the batteries, ran into the living room to turn on the TV, and sat down in what he called his armchair, but which had in fact been a very comfortable old chair of my mother's. I sat on the sofa, which was uncomfortable. The evening didn't unfold well, we argued at length—and with growing anger—over not one but three remote controls. He knew, precisely, how to enter the numbers of the channels that played cartoons nonstop, he put in DVDs with an ease that got on my nerves. What's more, he didn't obey any pact. We watch cartoons for five minutes, he said at one point, then Grandpa gets to watch something he likes. I assented, but I quickly discovered that five minutes meant, for him, *always*, and so I resigned myself to dozing off in front of the cartoons. But then I suddenly remembered that a friend of mine was going to be on a talk show that very evening; he had to promote one of his books, and he'd asked to put one of my paintings on the cover. So without further discussion I took all the remote controls away from the child, I simply said: Your five minutes are up, any complaints and I turn it off. He didn't complain. He hunched down, glowering, on the armchair. I ignored his foul humor and flipped though various channels searching for the show that had invited my friend. I finally landed on the right one: There he was, I glimpsed him for a few seconds among the other guests. Since Mario was staring at the screen in silence, as soon as they went back to focus on my friend I said brightly:

—I just want to hear what this man says and then I'll let you watch some more cartoons, OK?

Silence.

I got comfortable on the sofa, I dropped the remote control to one side. Meanwhile there was the host, talking about the book, here was the cover. I said:

—See that? That's mine.

He asked quietly:

—The book?

—The painting reproduced on the cover. Tomorrow tell your teacher.

Abruptly raising his voice, he said:

—I don't like it.

—You don't like anything, Mario.

—I just like the yellow.

The yellow? I couldn't remember paying particular heed to any yellow, I didn't remember even using one. On the other hand I had no time to look: The cover disappeared, the host had asked my friend to speak.

—Quiet, I said to the child, who wanted to say something else. Now just sit and listen.

My friend began talking, but as usual Mario immediately violated my prohibition, he left the armchair, he climbed up on the sofa, he said god knows what. I didn't even answer him, at least I don't think I did, I wanted to hear if my friend was going to mention me. Around thirty years younger than I was, brilliant in his field, he was confident about his work, discussing it as if were the most important thing in the world. I'd never been able to cast such light on myself. I'd worked hard all my life and I'd always been ashamed of giving importance to what I did, I always hoped acclaim would come from others. My friend, meanwhile, was arguing that he'd altered an entire school of study in that book, and he did this without embarrassment, with conviction, so much so that the host was nodding in agreement, and the other guests were listening with interest. I wished they'd focus on the cover again, I hoped they'd mention me and that Mario would hear my name, Daniele Mallarico, and exclaim: They talked about you. Instead suddenly a cartoon came on, brightly colored, full of animals who were all experts at kung fu.

I whipped around, I burst out:

—Who said you could take over the remote, who said you could change the channel?

Mario was scared. He replied:

—I asked you, Grandpa, and you said yes.

I extended an angry arm and he immediately handed back the remote control. I tried to go back to my friend, muttering, disgruntled, all the while, but I couldn't remember the channel.

—You have to put in the number, the child said, agitated.

—Quiet.

I skipped from one channel to the next, I found the right one, but my friend wasn't on anymore. I threw the remote onto the sofa and said, with fake calm:

—Go to bed now, right away.

But I did nothing to see this command through. Instead I left the room, I roamed through the house, I turned on lights,

I heard myself muttering disjointed sentences in dialect. I was now not only spent to the point of instability, but unhappy, as if every unhappy moment in my life had decided to gather together in that house, in that moment. I went into the child's room, where my things were, tripping over the items strewn across the floor, toys upon toys, kicking away a few of them. I looked for my cigarettes, but it occurred to me that Betta would go ballistic if, upon her return, she smelled smoke, so I went out to the balcony.

The noise of the traffic hit me right away, along with the freezing cold air. I took one or two cautious steps outside, I inhaled smoke and coughed. It was a night without stars, even though the day had been clear, and the racket of the cars, the station, the loudspeakers, the trains, seemed incredibly bright, a swirl of headlights, taillights, illuminated glass, a red-whiteyellowblack noise. In spite of the cold I smoked the cigarette almost down to the filter. I stubbed it out on the railing, I let it fly down, I came back in.

The voices from the talk show still reverberated through the house, Mario hadn't gone back to cartoons. When I returned to the living room, I found him asleep on the sofa. He slept soundly, and I brushed his sweaty forehead with my lips.

6.

As I carried the child's limp body in my arms, down the dark hallway, I felt a distressing bitterness inside me. I put him on the bed still dressed, without turning on the lights. All I did was take his shoes off. Leaving him there, I felt he'd retained my heat.

Once more, quickly, I crossed the rooms of the dark house—I had to learn how to feel the ghosts around me—orienting myself by the glimmer in the living room, where a light had stayed on, along with the chatter of the television. I sat on the armchair previously occupied by Mario. I tried to focus on the TV but I was cold and tired, I didn't feel like watching anything, so I turned it off. I checked to see if the radiator in the living room was still on and I almost burned myself grazing it with my finger. Maybe the cold was coming from another room but I gave up trying to figure it out. I was still struggling to find the right light switches. I thought of Mario with a mixture of wonder and rancor; he'd noticed my incompetence right away. Yes, he was just like his father, sprung from centuries of the most scholarly of scholars, pedantic, persnickety. He had nothing of my family, nothing of me, not the looks, not the behavior. The child was made of foreign matter, chromosomes hailing from some other place, hidden molecules crammed with information that was obscure to me, perhaps hostile, going back thousands of thousands of years. I thought, with a sad sense of irony, that even my ghosts would have been insulted by that child, he was hooked up to some other genetic motor. They were furious with me because, having banished them in early adolescence, I'd turned weak. Young Master, they were saying, you wanted to become a gentleman of fine sentiments, and look where you've ended.

I shooed those images away and got up, groaning, from the armchair. I forced myself to wander again through the house, but this time turning on all the lights. Still on the threshold of adolescence I was seeing—if I moved in the dark, or in half-light—relatives of my mother and father whom I'd known or seen only in photographs. They'd died during the war, I was sure about that, and yet there they were, standing in various corners of the house, hidden behind a door, hidden behind a closet. When I spotted them they made signs telling me to be quiet, they resorted to winking, they laughed without sound. Then that season had passed, but now I remembered more dead people than I did as a child—so many of my friends and

acquaintances were now deceased, after dreadful illnesses—
and my anxiety had also centupled, so much so that at times,
in Milan, I'd wake up suddenly, convinced that there were
thieves or murderers in the house, and I would wander sleep-
less through the rooms, shuddering when I thought a trick of
the light, cast on the wall by the wavering foliage of the trees
in the courtyard, was a hideous presence. Then I'd think, what
was there to worry about? I should be suffering more from
melancholy than anxiety: I've lived most of my life, and now I,
too, am coming close to dying. Mario would be the one to find
me behind a cupboard door, or in the dark corners of this
house. The brain, with its circuit of emotions, was able to set
so many semblances in motion. The child wasn't afraid of the
dark but maybe, after our days of living together, he'd be afraid
of my apparitions.

I was sleepy, without even the slightest energy to work. I
made sure I was the only possible ghost wandering through the
house, that there were no thieves motivated by poverty, or mur-
derous thugs from the camorra. I shut off the gas, I secured the
dead bolt, two turns. I have to keep it shut all day tomorrow, I
told myself, the knob is high up and even if he got up on a chair,
Mario, a miniature *homo faber*, could reach it with his hands,
open up, and go off to his pretend friend on the first floor. I
backtracked, turning off one light after another behind me. As
I finally got into bed, careful not to trip over any toys, I thought
I could relax. All the ghosts were in the old house of my adolescence. That house—now as I was drifting off I realized it—
formed a big frame around the one Mario and I were in. I saw
them and I would draw them, soon, but from a space where I
felt safe. The old house and the current one weren't able to flow
into each other. When I turned on the lights here, the ghosts
there fell into darkness; and when, as I'd done just now, I
turned off the very last light in this house and pulled the covers
over my head, the rooms from long ago suddenly lit up and

their inhabitants—all of them, made of everything about me that I'd gotten rid of—offered themselves up like an inert substance that, according to aging fantasies of an aging science, would have quickly turned to muck, alive and insatiable.

7.

The second day was the toughest. By five I was already up. I checked on Mario who, dressed as I'd left him, and under the covers to boot, was all sweaty. Since the radiators weren't on yet, I feared that uncovering him would cause him to catch cold, and so I limited myself to freeing his feet, still sheathed in socks, and his shoulders, protected by a sweater. Tonight—I told myself—I have to get him to put on his pajamas before watching television. Then I went to the living room and worked decently on images of the double house, the present one and the one from the past, one inside the other. All told, I thought it was useful to free myself from James's story, and so I aimed for illustrations inspired by the apartment of my adolescent years, and by my own ghosts. I asked myself, What did I know about New York at the end of the 1800s? I'll use Naples and create, between the present house and the one from the past, a transparent cavity. I'll put kids in it, lots of kids, all of them touching, like a long chain of Siamese twins: raised in poverty, lacking qualities, kids who don't hide their faces in the shadows or behind their hands, they don't need to, they're incomplete bodies in and of themselves, panting without mouths or eyes, scratching with maimed limbs, lacerating themselves with the pressing need to lengthen, grow, gain identity.

I followed this route and dared, in the sketches, to use extreme colors, strident tones. I thought of Mario again: Nothing I'd done had impressed him, from the very start. He'd frowned at the illustrations in the book of fairy tales, and he'd called my painting on TV ugly. But he was four years old, I was certain that he was repeating what Saverio thought of my work, maybe even Betta. Only his praise of my yellow belonged to him, and it had seemed real to me, an unbridled declaration. At a certain point I heard him moving around the house, first in the bathroom, then in the kitchen. I gave it a finishing touch, then one more: In the end I went to see what he was up to.

I surprised him standing on a kitchen chair. He'd turned on the gas, he'd put on the water for my tea, and his milk. I didn't want to begin the day by scolding him. I asked:

—Did you sleep well?

—Yeah, did you?

—Me too.

—It's easy sleeping with clothes on, that way I'm already ready.

—You still need to wash and put on clean clothes.

—Have you washed up yet?

—No.

—Did you go pee?

—Yes, did you go?

—Yes.

—Turn off the gas.

He turned it off and suggested, hesitantly:

—Can I not wash today?

I poured his milk into a cup and put a bag into the teapot.

—Okay.

—I'll wash up when Mom gets back.

—Okay.

—And always sleep with my clothes on.

—No, not that.

He grew sad for an instant, then perked up, and after that breakfast went smoothly. It was difficult, on the other hand, getting him to accept that I needed to close myself up in the bathroom for my ablutions.

—What are ablutions?

—Taking a shower.

—And what do I do while you're in the bathroom?

—Whatever you want.

He thought about it, he seemed torn.

—Can I take a shower, too?

I sent him off to pick out clean underwear and I stuck him under the stream of water while he, in his prescriptive way, reminded me: You'll die if you go in the water after eating. But given I didn't appear concerned with saving his life, he started to jump up and down, dance, spit water, shout out: It's boiling! So I dried him off, I dressed him and chased him out saying, now it's my turn. Can I stay? he asked. I said no and for a few minutes I heard him in the hallway, jumping around, humming. Then suddenly he started to jiggle the door handle persistently, to kick the wood, to scream: Grandpa, I see you through the lock; or: Let me in, I need to pee, I need to poo. I yelled: Be quiet and behave yourself, stop that right away. I hastened to dry off and get dressed, then I opened the door wide.

—I was quiet, I behaved myself, he said.

—It was about time.

—When will I have a willy like yours?

—You really looked through the lock?

—Yeah.

—You'll have a much nicer willy than mine.

—When?

—Soon.

The doorbell rang emphatically and we looked at each other, uncertain. It wasn't even eight o'clock. He advised me:

—Put the big knife for meat on the table by the front door.

—Why? Does Dad get the knife every time they ring the bell?

—No, Mom gets it when Dad isn't here.

—Us guys are tough, we don't need a knife.

—I'm scared.

—There's nothing to be scared of.

I opened the door. I found myself standing in front of a man in his fifties, skinny, medium height, his face rather creased, his hair thinning. I saw that he had some toys in his hands—a red truck, a plastic sword—and deduced that it must have been the father of the boy on the first floor. I assumed a cordial expression and said:

—Thank you, there was no need to go out of your way, there's no hurry.

The man grew timid. Sounding pained, he said:

—My wife wouldn't let up.

—Wives are like that.

—But Professor Cajuri goes overboard.

—What does she do?

—She doesn't realize that my son is six years old, and since he doesn't have the same toys Mario does, sometimes he hides them so that he can play with them on his own.

—And let him play, Mario is happy to leave them for a few days, right, Mario?

The child, clinging to one of my legs, said yes theatrically. The man said:

—I know, but the professor doesn't get it. So allow me the courtesy of suggesting that the kid needs to stop lowering down the bucket with toys inside it, and he can't come over anymore. There are no crooks in our house. The thieves here are the ones who spend money buying a bunch of toys.

—Now you're going too far. My daughter works, she doesn't steal.

—I work, too. But your daughter says we steal, and that's not right. Bye, Mario, and sorry. You, we liked.

He handed him the toys and the child took them, but the truck fell out. I said:

—Come in, I'll make you cup of coffee.

—Let's just say I accepted. Have a nice day.

He left without taking the elevator, going down the stairs. It was clear he'd carried out a task he hadn't chosen for himself and that he'd done it unwillingly. He seemed like a nice guy, I'd have gladly talked to him about what the city had been like when I was a boy, about my youth before I'd left Naples, and about how once everything—the good and the bad—seemed like a reflection of the place you were born and how these days, instead, everything—the good and the bad—seems written in the depths of our flesh. Even though I had work to do and it was eight in the morning, I felt like I needed to have a meandering conversation with an adult. I was sick of being alone all the time with the child. Mario picked up the truck and shouted at him:

—I'll send them down to Attilio in the bucket.

—You're not sending down anything, I said. Take your stuff to your room and stay there: I don't want to be disturbed today.

8.

I don't know how long I spent arranging sketches and drawings of those days in order to come up with a version with ten convincing illustrations. I worked hard, sure, as if I really had the old house, down to the last detail, before my eyes: its frightened or aggressive inhabitants, a tangle of young bodies deformed by pressure against the transparent wall separating myself today from everything I might have been. Those beings crept along, leapt, twisted, fought, they tore each other apart, and to define them I plundered, from illustration to illustration, all my experiences. But I never really let myself go. I was afraid of forgetting about Mario, who was playing at the end of the hallway, and I was afraid above all of forgetting myself. So pleasure never prevailed over the toil of it. I simply relied on the diligent effort I knew I was capable of, and when I stopped, I realized I'd slaved away only to be able to say: Here we are, the plates are ready, more or less, and I've made them to my liking. But I ruled out the possibility that the publisher would like them.

I was tired. I stared at the big painting hanging in front of me. When had I done it? Over twenty years ago. There had been a discreet consensus surrounding me in those days, charging me with new energy, and almost as if corroborated by that consensus, everything came easily, and this generated further consensus. What I had before my eyes belonged to that happy time: two meters wide, one meter high, just a red and a blue, pure pools of color spreading on the wood, inside of which I'd put, in a little nook I'd created, a metal cowbell. I left the table and moved to a corner. I hadn't pulled up the blinds yet, I always liked working with the lights on. The electric light poured down from the lamp; it made the edge of the bell sparkle, radiating a shiny arc that moved from the red and ended up in the blue.

For a while it all seemed well-conceived. But soon enough the satisfaction struck me as the effect of melancholy. Was it memorable work, or mere testimony from a season when my body felt vigorous, fulfilled? I started to detect a thousand flaws. I slowly convinced myself that not only had I grown old, but so had that work. The painting then struck me as a piece of wood with an ugly smear on it: What was that golden dust that I'd put along the edges like a rectangular halo, what was the point of digging out, on the colored plank, a little spot for an actual object? Fashions, I thought, sadly, wear out, leaving behind the futile traces of those who upheld them. I left my corner, I lifted up the blinds. A wan light came into the room, the sky was cloudy again. I went back to the painting. In natural light everything seemed to get much worse: The red now looked like deadened tissue, the blue an infected pool. Ugly, insignificant, both that pathetic plank and all my work, even though I'd liked them, even if they'd met with some success. Perhaps I should have inserted, now, among my ghosts, the shadows of those paintings I believed I'd made but, thinking about it with some distance, hadn't made at all. There was a veritable nucleus in me that wanted to split apart and release, onto the world, forms never before seen. But I—that is to say my individuality as time had defined it, that is to say, all the little lessons I'd learned and the languages I'd assimilated—had only been able to produce works like that piece of wood with a cowbell. Better Mario's little drawings, proudly framed by his parents alongside my painting, and throughout the room. I glanced at mountains, fields, huge flowers, indecipherable animals, human beings with big ears, all of it obtained by the uncontrolled strokes of a crayon, all of it in green and blue. A child's scribbles, Betta, too, made them when she was little. All kids do. I felt so upset that I would have given almost anything to start all over again, and be someone else. I needed air, I said to myself. I opened the windows, the door to the veranda. Then I left the living room and went to air out the rest of the house.

I pushed apart the kitchen windows, I went into Betta's study, then Mario's room: The pent-up air was giving me a headache and I didn't want to add one malady to another. The child had stayed put the whole time, disciplined, among his toys. I'd heard him while he talked to his action figures, he made noises with his mouth, he shouted commands, he brought forth the shrill yet honey-coated voices one heard on television. When I came into the room he was seated on the floor, making a monstrous horned animal fly through the air, supporting it with one hand while clutching some sort of superhero with the other. As soon as he realized I was there he stopped himself for a moment. He threw a glance my way to make sure I wasn't there to prevent him from doing something, or to reproach him, and then he went on playing as if I weren't there.

I opened the balcony door, setting down a chair so that it wouldn't slam shut in the wind, and above all so that Mario wouldn't find me locked outside. I made our two beds, sloppily, and I put the dirty clothes in a sack. But now I couldn't help myself; I couldn't not look, at least askance, at the countless little drawings hung up in that room, too. He'll grow up—I thought—and who knows who he'll think he is, or what he's destined for. And how could it be otherwise, if his parents did nothing but praise him, even when he was only four years old: Look at all these sheets of paper, all with the same colored figures, same as in the living room, the hallway; Betta and Saverio didn't throw anything away, they were convinced that every one of his trifles was anointed by rosy-fingered genius. I grew increasingly glum. I tried to ward off my foul humor, attributing it to my physical decline, but it didn't help. And yet it certainly wasn't the first time that I'd suffered a crisis of faith. But I felt, in front of those drawings, that there was something more—how to say it—organic, something that threw me and shook me to my core. Thank goodness Mario stepped in. He stopped playing, he came up to me with the superman in one hand and the monster in the other. He said, pointing to the wall with the hand that clutched the monster:

—That one's dark, Grandpa, do you like it?

—I like them all.

—Not true. You said I made them too light.

—I was kidding: You said my drawings were too dark so I said yours were too light.

—I didn't know you were kidding.

—It's okay, you can't know everything.

—So will I get good like you?

—I hope not.

—See how you don't like my drawings?

—I like them a lot. They're a child's drawings, and everyone likes what a child draws.

—The teacher says mine are the nicest.

—The teacher knows little or nothing and is wrong about a whole series of things.

—You're wrong, he said, and he struck my leg with the monster, softly, to emphasize his objection.

—Ouch, I said, playing with him, and gave him a poke with two fingers on his shoulder.

He smiled, he looked happy. Gotcha, he exclaimed, and he hit me more forcefully on the leg. Then he started shouting, laughing: Gotcha, gotcha, gotcha, and each time he'd hit me with his awful stuffed beast, always harder, rapid fire. Until he said: Die, die, and I tried to parry the blows, they were hurting me now. But he also struck the back of the hand I was protecting myself with, I felt the cuts from the monster's horns. I seized his arm as he was about to strike again:

—Stop it, you've hurt me.

He said softly, his voice now conciliatory:

—Gotcha.

—Well, don't get me again, look what you've done.

I showed him the long cut on my hand. He stared at the furrow of blood and said quietly, to justify himself: You never want to play with me. Then he added, struggling to contain the sudden quiver in his chin: I'll give you a little kiss and you'll feel better.

I let him give me the kiss so that he wouldn't cry again. Now my left leg also hurt. My buttock, too.

—Feel better? he asked.

—I feel better, but don't ever do that again. Do you know where the stuff is, to clean this up?

He knew, naturally. He asked me to follow him into the

bathroom, and he showed me where the hydrogen peroxide was kept.

—Do you know how to open the bottle? he asked.

—Of course I know.

—I don't.

—Try, just for once, not to learn.

I sent him out and closed the door. I checked my leg and my buttock, where there were small cuts as well, and I disinfected them. With old age came the fear of even a scrape; I pictured infections, sepsis, being rushed to the hospital. I doubt it was the fear of death, rather, it was the nuisance of illness, the bother of messing up one's daily routine. Or maybe it was the terror of a prolonged death: I preferred yielding to a single blow, an instant, never breathing again.

—You outside?

—Yeah.

—Don't move.

—Okay.

I could tell he was worried that he'd done something irreparable, and I was ashamed for having lost my patience. When I came out I told him:

—Let's eat, now, and then we'll work together.

—We're going to draw?

—Yes.

—In the same room?

—Of course, how else would we work together?

9.

I tried to be as affectionate as possible during lunch. And the child also took care not to jeopardize our future collaboration. So for starters, instead of dictating how to set the table, he let me do it. And he even managed to keep his mouth shut about using the microwave, necessary for defrosting the food Sally had prepared. He only persisted, prudently, in asking how we'd be working together—he, too, used that verb—and for how long. I replied that we'd work together for a long time, a very long time, until it grew dark, and I assured him—he'd asked me, pausing awkwardly between the words—that in addition to his paints he'd be able to use mine, though only for a short time. I realized that it meant the world to him to pretend to collaborate with me, surely more than playing with the ladder or reducing me to a horse again, and I began to feel as if I'd set a trap for myself. I hoped that he'd get tired of it soon, before I did and, given the frazzled state of my nerves, flew into a rage, forgetting that he was four years old.

Before holing up in the living room we went to his room to get paper and paints. The child wanted to give me a hand, as if we were walking through a dangerous forest and he had to make sure I didn't get lost. I noticed that I'd left the balcony open and I was about to close it, but he called me, I had to help him put his work supplies in a bag. When we finally moved over to the living room he held my hand again, and I understood that the real intention behind that gesture was to keep me inside that sweet, promising atmosphere.

Once we were in the room he made sure that his chair was as close to mine as possible, and we sat down. But then he seemed to remember something urgent and said: I'm going to get the pillows. I asked why he needed them and he got into a lather explaining to me how uncomfortable he was, and that in order to sit properly he needed pillows under his bottom. He disappeared, he didn't come back, and I felt alone, rattled by the gray sky, the drowsy light, the little cuts on my leg and buttock, the sting of the red streak on my hand. When, reluctantly, I was about to go see where he'd ended up, he came back in a hurry carrying one of the little blue pillows that his mother arranged on the floor so that one wouldn't catch cold. He placed it on the chair, climbed up, and, after determining that he was comfortable, asked if he could use my sheets of paper, which seemed better suited than his. I allowed him this. Only then did I lean against the back of the chair, stretching my legs out under the table, and while Mario patiently waited for me to assign him a task, I reexamined the work I'd done in the past few days.

Page after page, I was increasingly disappointed. I already suspected that I hadn't given it my best shot; the ten plates that I'd fine-tuned seemed something other that what I'd thought I'd done. I tried to calm down, to not blow my dissatisfaction out of proportion, and without thinking I turned to the child, who was looking over my arm. I needed an opinion and he, sitting there beside me, was the only one who could provide it. I asked him if he liked the illustrations. I wasn't kidding, I was really asking, and it was a moment of absolute truth that amazed even me.

My request caused Mario to turn beet red. Instead of looking at the illustrations he looked at me, I think, to figure out if our game had begun. I pushed the pile of sheets in front of him, one on top of the other, in the order I wanted to suggest to the publisher. He stared at the first one, seeming to drink it up with his eyes, an antiquated metaphor that I've always loved: People and things dissolve, turn to liquid, and the eyes become mouth and throat, changing the irreducible world into a potion. The child said:

—You made this one light, see all the yellow?

I looked, puzzled, first at him, then at the illustration, and then I realized that he was right. Unintentionally, opposing the stylistic bent rooted in me by now, I'd used a lot of yellow, or at least gone for the effect that Mario called yellow. Had I been looking for his approval? I felt like laughing, and the child could tell. He asked gravely:

—Did I say something wrong?

—No, I reassured him, no, go on, tell me what you think. Grandpa is happy to hear what you have to say.

But that same moment the phone rang. What a pain, I said, and the child agreed with me, he said: Don't go, it's those guys that cheat you over the phone, Dad always shouts at them to leave him alone. The phone rang again, once, twice, three times, four, keeping us both is suspense. I'll get it, I said, and Mario advised me: Yell at them, that way they get scared and won't bug us anymore.

I went to the kitchen. The cordless was missing from its base, I'd left it on the counter next to the sink. I said hello. It wasn't someone who scraped out a living by palming off all sorts of crap over the phone. It was Betta.

Didn't you say you were going to call at dinnertime? I asked, walking down the hallway with the cordless at my ear.

—Yes, but tonight I can't, Saverio's giving his talk at seven and after that we're booked solid.

—Things better between you two?

—Are you kidding? They're worse. He's so uptight about his talk that he's starting to rant and rave. He says that while he's in the room going over his paper, I'm hooking up with my friend. The asshole's so paranoid that a few minutes ago he was on the verge of hitting me in public.

—Hitting you?

—Yes.

—Tell him if he dares, I'll kill him.

—You'll kill him? A minute ago she was lamenting, but now she burst out laughing. Do you feel OK, Dad?

—I feel great, tell him so.

She was laughing hysterically now, the way she used to when she was little.

—OK, she promised, half choking on the words. I'll report back: My father said if you lay a hand on me he'll kill you.

She couldn't control herself. The mere fact of putting in words to something that, in that moment, I believed I'd have done with ease, seemed unthinkable to her. I tossed in, seriously:

—Leave him, Betta. You're still young, smart, beautiful. Find someone else who's right for you, have a son with him, no, wait, a daughter.

She kept laughing, but now it wasn't genuine.

—You're insane. How's it going with Mario?

—He said you shouldn't bother us.

—Good. What are you doing?

—We're drawing.

—Have you seen how good he is?

—Oh, sure.

—Say hi to him, tell him I love him, we'll talk tomorrow.

I went back to Mario. His opinion really did mean a lot, even if it made me feel stupid. I discovered that he, in the meantime, had looked at all the plates, and then neatly piled them to his right. Well? I asked. He didn't say anything. He wanted to know, first, who was on the phone, if it was one of the swindlers his father would get mad at. When I told him I'd spoken with Betta, he was upset, complaining that I should have called him. I struggled to convince him that his mother was busy, I struggled to turn him back to the illustrations.

—Don't you want to play anymore?

—I do.

—Well then, how are my drawings?

—Beautiful.

—Really?

—But they're a little scary.

—They *have* to be scary, it's a ghost story.

He shook his head, skeptical, and went back to looking at the sheets, one after another, searching for one in particular. He found it and showed it to me.

—Who's the guy sitting here?

—The hero of the story.

—What's his name?

—Spencer Brydon.

—Is he the ghost?

—The ghosts are the ones behind the glass.

—Are they crying?

—They're shouting.

—They have holes for mouths, they don't even have teeth. At least give them some teeth.

—It's fine the way it is. What do you think of the yellow?

He thought about it, then said:

—This yellow is ugly.

I got annoyed, there was no yellow where he was pointing. Was he still playing around? It was unbearable that he was giving pretend answers. On the other hand, what did I expect, I was the one making the outlandish request. Asking a snotty-nosed kid to judge my work, asking him because I needed reassurance, enough, enough. I cut it short. OK, I said, now you make your drawing and I'll make mine. But he didn't like this idea, and we talked it over awhile. He'd gotten it into his head that we'd both draw, on the same sheet of paper, and it was tough persuading him that we each had to devote ourselves to our own work without bothering each other.

—What do I draw? he asked, in a terrible mood.

—Whatever you want.

—I'll draw what you draw.

—OK.

—I'm drawing a ghost.

—OK.

—That way we work together.

—OK.

I was prepared to raise my voice were he to hinder my concentration, but there was no need. After a few seconds I lost

track of him, nor did he do a thing to remind me of his existence. Of course I sensed Mario beside me, but this, all told,
seemed a good thing. I didn't need to worry about him, I'd be
able to work all afternoon touching up or reworking whatever
didn't convince me, and maybe I'd even rid myself of the torment for good. If the publisher still didn't find it to his liking,
so what, I'd come up with other ways to distract myself in old
age. My life had run its course, I'd done what I could do, what
I knew how to do. Whether it was a lot, a little, or nothing,
what did it matter? I'd devoted all my time to that vocation,
and now the pleasure, along with the time, had also slipped
away. My hand always got tired, but the fulfillment had once
been such that I wouldn't notice. Now I couldn't ignore the icy
numbness in my fingers. It whittled my imagination, it even
overcame my stubborn self-discipline. I couldn't take the exer-
tion anymore, I could tell. I quit, pushing the paper away.
Once more I looked at my red-blue painting with the cowbell,
then I turned to Mario. He was bent over the paper, almost
touching it with his half-open lips, his nose. Are you done? I
asked. He didn't answer. I asked again and he looked at me
blankly. Yes, he said, then added:

—Are you done, Grandpa?

I was the one who didn't reply this time. He'd lifted his face
from the paper and I saw the drawing, the colors. Nothing to
compare to the little houses and meadows framed in the living
room, the hordes of animals displayed in his room. On the
boy's sheet of paper was evidence of an extraordinary mimetic
ability, a natural harmony of composition, a fanciful sense of
color. He'd drawn me, utterly recognizable: me now, me today.
And yet I emanated horror, I really was my ghost.

—Have you made other drawings like this? I asked.

—You don't like it?

—It's beautiful. Do you have any more drawings like this one?

—No.

—Tell me the truth.

—I did.

I pointed to the sheets taped to the walls of the room.

—Those aren't as nice as this one.

—Not true, the teacher likes them a lot, so do Mom and Dad.

—So why did you draw like this?

—I copied how you draw.

I took the sheet of paper from him and looked at it. I reeled. A violent shove had sent me from the center of the world to its very edges. I remembered another blow just as strong, something I'd felt as a boy when I'd discovered, at once amazed and terrified, what I was really capable of. But whereas the earlier shove had led me to an increasingly headstrong belief in my absolute uniqueness and centrality—I'd dreamed up such outsized ambitions—the shove from Mario's drawing, I felt, could annihilate me. I reacted by intervening, correcting something. The child nearly shouted with enthusiasm:

—Great, Grandpa, it's prettier that way.

As soon as I heard those words— it's prettier that way—I pulled back the black tip of the pencil, as if, with it, I were harming not the paper but Mario. I looked away. The lines and colors were poisoning me. I said softly:

—Yes, we've really done great work today.

He grew serious. He assumed a haughty tone and, looking at the illustration that I'd been working on until a minute ago, murmured:

—Really great. Yours is quite bright.

—Let's sign them.

He got confused. He said:

—I don't know how, can you help me?

—No, you have to sign in your own way.

—But if I make a mistake I'll ruin it for you.

—You want to sign my drawing?

His face darkened.

—We worked together.

—OK. You sign mine and I'll sign yours?

He shouted out yes with excessive glee and I passed my sheet over to him. Filled with tension he wrote, at the bottom, with a red marker, in irregular block letters: Mario. I was getting ready to sign his drawing with the same marker when he stopped me, saying: Not with the red, with green. I signed Grandpa in green, he was right, it made more sense with different colors. But meanwhile the humiliation was building deep within me. It was an unbearable sentiment, and to get rid of it I exclaimed: Now that the game's over, let's destroy everything. I pointed to my illustration, the one he'd just signed, and then, since he was looking at me, unsure, his eyes somewhere between joy and worry—I took another and tore it up into tiny pieces.

—Just kidding? he asked softly.

—Just kidding.

He emitted a high-pitched shriek and helped tear up all my work with the reckless merriment with which children demolish what they've patiently put together with the help of adults. He was tearing, tossing the pieces into the air, shrieking and laughing. When he was about to rip apart his own drawing, I stopped him, seizing his arm.

—Hey, he complained.

I took away the sheet of paper and said:

—Not this. This one is a present for Grandpa, who will keep it safe.

But he clearly considered the game far too entertaining and, smiling at me, his face defiant, tried to snatch away the sheet. I pushed him away, he laughed. I hadn't understood a thing about that child, he seemed well-mannered but he wasn't. He attacked me again, I attacked back. Since he wasn't able to take the drawing away from me, he started throwing pencils, markers, paints, my albums, all over the room, and he accompanied the throwing of each thing by mirthfully shouting: Just kidding. I tried to get him to stop, saying the game was over, but I couldn't, and in the end I took him off the chair, from his pillow, and ordered him:

—Now put everything back in its place, immediately, before we start arguing again.

He stopped himself, and in an instant he went from being happy to sulking.

—You help, too.

—It's your fault, so you're going to do it alone.

—You're the one who told me to rip up the drawings.

—True, but I didn't tell you to make this mess.

—We were just kidding.

—I don't want to talk about it.

—You're mean.

—I am. And I forbid you to come out of this room until you've picked up all my stuff and put it where it belongs.

What was happening to me? I fought the urge to threaten him; my hand was tense, an inch from his cheek, prepared to strike. To avoid this I left the living room, slamming the door behind me with such force that a sliver of paint detached itself from the jamb.

10.

I went to the kitchen to look for my cigarettes and found them next to the sink. I felt that something had happened in the living room, something definitive, but I needed to take a break to calm down. I resisted the cigarette, better a camomile tea. I threw open cupboards and drawers, but at random, I didn't know if there was any in the house, and I didn't want to ask that live feral puppet. Good god, what had he done, how

could he have known, seated beside me, just inches away? I
needed a place to think about it calmly.

I went to the bathroom, I urinated with difficulty, I came
out. I felt chilled by the air, I didn't remember if I'd closed the
glass door in Mario's room. I didn't think so, the child had distracted me. I went to check: The balcony was still open. I
moved the chair that blocked the door and looked outside. I
could still see a little purple light at the base of the blackened
sky above the office district. I then discovered that the bucket
was missing, the cord was hanging over the railing. Once again
the blood rose to my head. When Mario had come to get the
pillow he hadn't been able to resist, and in spite of every prohibition he'd stopped to lower the bucket and send toys to his
friend. Sooner or later Attilio's father would come back to
complain, or worse, it would be the wife. I was angry, I stepped
cautiously onto the balcony. It was windy, I pulled up the cord,
nauseated from the slight vertigo. The bucket, thank goodness,
was still full of toys. I heard Mario behind me, who cried out
happily:

—Grandpa, I'm gonna play a trick on you.

I turned around, I told him:

—Don't come out, it's cold.

He didn't come out. He pushed the glass door as hard as he
could and locked me outside.

CHAPTER THREE

1.

I did nothing. For a great many seconds I stood there against the railing with the cord in my hands, the bucket still swaying in the void, my head turned to look at the white door frame and the long slab of double-paned glass. The noise of the traffic grew unbearable, it silenced every other sound. I could neither hear the child nor see him. The day's light had dwindled to hues too weak to spread through the room. I abruptly let go of the cord. I moved, slowly, from the outer edges of the balcony and finally distinguished Mario. He wasn't moving. He stood stock-still, his stature slight in the lower half of the glass door, his hands still pressed against the glass, his eyes stealthy. I didn't say anything, I felt numb. I only pressed my hands against the glass, as if I were a projection of Mario's motionless pose, and I pushed emphatically, convinced that it was the child who prevented me from getting back inside, and that my strength was enough to crush his own. The door didn't budge so much as a millimeter, and I finally started to panic for real. My movements turned frenetic and, now gasping, I started to exert an irrational amount of pressure with my entire body against the glass. Then I gave up. I was outside, and Mario was in.

I managed not to shout, even though in that moment the aversion I felt toward Mario was stinging my eyes. Instead I got upset, silently, at Saverio. The imbecile had installed a door without an outside handle; his only concerns were to keep out the sounds that would bother his sleeping son, and thieves from coming into the room. What's more, even though the door was faulty, he, consumed by the itch to torment my daughter, had never gotten around to replacing it or even getting it fixed. How could Betta have lived with a man like this for so long, and even have a child with him? I bent down to Mario's height. Now all I saw were his extremely pallid hands against the glass; darkness had completely devoured the sky, the balcony, the room, the child. I knocked lightly with my knuckles, I forced myself to smile.

—Nice trick, I said, speaking loudly. Now, please, can you turn the lights on?

—Right away, Grandpa.

—Don't run, don't hurt yourself.

Even the little hands vanished, but only for an instant. The room burst into light that flooded the balcony, and this calmed me down. The child came back in a hurry, he was excited.

—Now what do I do?

That, indeed, was the problem: what to do.

—Sit down on the floor.

—And you on the balcony?

—Sure, I agreed, and with a bit of strain I crouched down next to the glass door.

—And now?

—Wait a minute.

I needed to think and, above all, measure my words. I didn't want him to feel the gravity of what he'd done, to get scared. He asked:

—Can you see me, Grandpa?

—Of course I see you.

—I see you, too. Should we say hi?

He waved at me with his hand to make sure I was in a good mood, and I waved back. But this didn't satisfy him. He pounded the glass, smiling, and I pounded back, smiling at him. I looked into his eyes. His shining pupils reflected little figurines of myself, a plaything that, just a little while ago, had passed miraculously through his hands, becoming a drawing that had left me speechless. What a tiny organism he was; and yet, what a world, what a wealth of words it already contained. He fettered them so as to give the impression of knowing perfectly what they meant, and yet he didn't know a thing. Every aspect of him was like this. He didn't even know what he'd drawn and colored a while back. Mario was just a small segment of a living substance whose potential—as is the case for anyone—was still compressed and waiting to develop. In the course of a couple of decades, for argument's sake, he'd put a damper on the greater part of himself—a vast tract he would cease to tread—and he would run behind some flash that would then be called *my destiny*. Mario, I said, rapping my knuckles against the glass, and he instantly lit up with interest, he couldn't wait to receive an order. So, I asked, Did you know that I can't get back into the house? Of course he knew—*I know, Grandpa*—but he didn't see a problem with it. Now let's play a little, he said, and then you'll come back in. Evidently he had an undetermined epoch of fun and games in mind—him on one side of the glass, me on the other—that would end when he got bored, and then I would come back into the apartment.

—Mario, I countered, if someone doesn't open the door for me I can't get back in.

—Sally will let you in.

—Sally comes tomorrow morning.

—So we'll play until tomorrow morning.

—Tomorrow morning is a ways off, we can't play that long.

—Do you have to work?

—Yes.

—You work too much, Grandpa. Let's play now, and then Dad will let you in.

—Dad gets back the day after tomorrow and the day after tomorrow is farther off than tomorrow morning.

—Then I'll let you in. Now tell me what we should do.

I was on the verge of losing control. The only thing that stopped me was the feeling that I had my cell phone in my pants pocket, but all I found there were a pack of cigarettes and matches. Who knew where the cell phone was, it had been a while since I'd used it. The last call I'd received—or that I'd been aware of, since normally I kept the ringer off—had been the publisher's. The child pounded hard against the glass, he couldn't stand it when I got distracted. Maybe I was making a mistake, maybe I should have terrorized him, made him realize the mess he'd gotten us into. But by that point I'd assumed that faux-affectionate tone and I kept using it.

—Mario, I said, do you know where the house phone is?

He was all aflutter.

—The cordless?

—The cordless.

—Sure I know.

—Can you get it?

—Yes.

—Without climbing on a chair?

—Yes.

He was about to run off. I rapped my knuckles on the glass:

—Wait.

I told him that he first had to do something else: get a piece of paper that was on the shelf next to the gas burners, and bring it to me.

—Quickly?

—No, without running.

As soon was I was alone I felt cold and I realized I was in slippers and a light pullover. But soon I'd be back in the house. On the sheet of instructions, Betta had left me some numbers just in case. Mario was so adept with phones and remote controls that it would be easy enough to get him to dial one of those numbers and ask for help. I looked down into the courtyard: It was a dark well, none of the windows, none of the balconies, stacked one on top of the other, emitted a glimmer. The street to my left, meanwhile, was a wide canal, thick with traffic, brightly lit, running from the lights of the station and festively flowing into strings of red taillights and headlights both creeping at a snail's pace in opposite directions. The clamor of voices, the drone of impatient motors, was violent. I felt weaker than usual, and it wasn't because of the physical exhaustion, it was Mario's astonishing drawing. Not even the distress of my situation could chase it away entirely.

The child rushed back, banging happily against the glass. He placed the piece of paper against it with both his hands. I crouched down and took off my glasses. Turn it around, I said. He turned it around. Among the numbers Betta had written down was Sally's, and I felt relieved. I asked him to leave the sheet on the floor and go get the cordless. He replied, with some uncertainty:

—I already went.

—Well then?

—It's not in its place.

—What do you mean?

—*You* didn't put it back.

The anxiety reared up. My fault, it was true, I'd talked to Betta at lunchtime and then I must have gotten distracted. What a scatterbrain, I did one thing and thought of another, life was seeping out. I tried to concentrate, but the child was fretting, he kept asking, banging on the glass: Grandpa, now what do we do? Now, I said to myself, I have to retrace my steps. I'd first needed to use the cordless the night before. Betta had called and I'd talked to her, roaming through the house. Then we'd said bye and I'd put the phone back in its place, in the kitchen at any rate. In fact when the call came today—*Grandpa, what should I do?*—that was where I'd found the device. But then the entire conversation with Betta had taken place in the hallway, this I clearly remembered. And in the end—*Grandpa, now what?*—I'd gone straightaway to Mario in the living room. The child struck the glass with both his hands to signal his impatience. I burst out, I shouted, Enough. He blinked, startled, and retracted his palms, facing out as if in surrender, from the glass. His mouth was half-open. I immediately regretted it. The last thing we needed was him crying again, or growing spiteful and refusing to collaborate. I smiled at him, and added: Sorry, Grandpa was thinking; but now I know where the phone is, I definitely left it in the living room. Go slowly, you'll find it on the table. He calmed down at once, and taking exceedingly slow steps toward the door, was swallowed up by the hallway.

There was some distant flash in the sky. I had to move a bit to fight off the cold. I stood up again but without moving from my place, I didn't trust that stone slab unnaturally perched over the void, vibrating from the traffic and the trains. To be honest there was nothing I trusted just then: not iron, not cement, not a single building in the city. The sense that each and every thing was precarious, a feeling Naples had conveyed to me since my adolescence, and which had prompted me to flee when I was twenty, was resurfacing. I dredged up the agglutination of construction and savage corruption, of looting and theft. I recalled how every second of life in that house, in that neighborhood, was signaled by my father's fingers on play-ing cards, by his rapacious need for a *thrill* that drove him to jeopardize our very survival. I fought with all my might to sep-arate myself from him, from all my ancestors, from the broken-down city, to prove that I was different. I'd derived strength from the assumption that I was exceptional. And now this child who carried who knows what species of hominid in his veins—this child who would grow to have large hands, thick legs, and would be pettily jealous like his father, falsely polite, in other words, be as far as possible from me—had suddenly, in plain sight, made a surprising drawing, and for no other reason than to imitate me. He'd pulled it forth like a trick, he'd wrested it from deep in his flesh, from who knows what nucleic acid, what phosphorus and nitrogen. And he'd thus revealed to me that he harbored the same force that I'd attributed to myself since I was young, considering it a sign of distinction. So it wasn't a matter of my being gifted. Rather, given that it appeared in him and maybe in anyone—even in the barista the other morning—it didn't define me as I'd always believed. I realized what had happened to me in the living room. Mario's drawing had snatched, from my body, the notion I'd had of myself. I shivered and nestled up to the glass, as if the light in the room could warm me up.

Clop clop clop, Mario was back. He was knocking the cordless against the glass, he'd found it. Bravo, I told him. I saw him incredibly excited, his cheeks were red, his eyes eager. He asked:

—What now, Grandpa?

2.

It appeared that things were looking up.

—Now take the sheet and hold it up for me against the glass, I said.

—Why?

—I need to memorize Sally's number.

He did as told. I softly uttered the number various times, trying to concentrate; then, fearing I'd forget it, I articulated it loudly to Mario and asked him to repeat it back to me. He shouted, happy that I was putting him to the task:

—Threethreefiveonezerotwooneninetwofive.

—Bravo, say it again.

—Threethreefiveonezerotwooneninetwofive.

—Now let's call.

The child sat down on the floor.

—You sit too, Grandpa.

I struggled to sit as close as possible to the glass. He repeated the numbers, talking to himself, pressing down on the keypad. A few seconds, then he shouted:

—Hi Sally, how are you? I'm good.

I sighed in relief, I hollered in turn:

—Tell her I'm locked out on the balcony and that she has to come right away with the keys.

But the child ignored me.

—Mom and Dad aren't back yet. I'm with Grandpa and we're doing great. But he slammed a door so hard it scared me. Now he's on the balcony and we're playing with the phone. Bye, Sally, bye, bye-bye.

He took the phone from his ear and looked at me:

—Should we make another phone call?

—Sally, I shouted, over his voice, Don't hang up, please. I'm on the balcony, I'm locked outside. I need help, Sally.

The child looked at me warily. I must have had an insane look on my face. He said:

—Sally's not there.

—She's not there because you hung up.

—I didn't hang up, he said quietly.

I sighed heavily:

—Call her back. Do you remember the number?

—Threethreefiveonezerotwooneninetwofive.

—Bravo. Dial it again.

He pressed a few buttons, too few for those numbers. He did it quickly, with false confidence, and part of me began feebly to ask if he'd been calling for real.

—Mario, please, redial the number and pay attention to what you're doing, I said.

His lower lip trembled.

—For real or for fun?

—For real. Let's go: 3-3-5.

He interrupted me:

—I don't know how to make a real phone call, Grandpa.

I said nothing, I was confused. I asked:

—You don't know the numbers?

—Just one, zero, and ten.

—And the remote control? You enter the numbers of the cartoon channels but you don't know how to use the phone?

—I'm little, he replied, and I saw that it pained him. But there was little to be done, he was indeed little and his parents, though they were mathematicians, had been lavish with words, not with numbers. When Mario needed the remote control to access the cartoon channels, he resorted to sight memory. But he couldn't manage the phone, he pushed buttons at random. Even now he was going at it, nervously, for appearance's sake. I watched his fingers skipping around and thought: Maybe someone will pick up in any case, and I was about to shout: Enough, listen to see if they say hello. But only then did I realize that the buttons emitted no sound, that the display was dark, that is, that the cordless was out of juice.

—Please, I said, go put the phone back in its place, immediately.

But perhaps because, due to the cold, it was hard to clearly pronounce the words, or perhaps because my request wasn't sufficiently peremptory, Mario didn't move.

—We're not going to play anymore? he asked, looking at the cordless.

—No.

—Because I don't know how to make a real call?

—No, because the phone's not working.

—But you can still play with a phone that doesn't work, me and Dad do it all the time: You're the one who doesn't want to play.

—Mario, stop complaining and go put the phone back in its place.

The child got up, but he left the phone on the floor. He said:

—It's your fault that it's not working, you're the one who didn't put it back in its place. Mom says you only ever think of yourself.

—Fine, but listen to me.

—No, I'm going to watch cartoons.

He left the room, even though I was hollering:

—Come back here, Mario, you've got to help me. Helping me is a game, too.

A minute passed, then two. I hoped he'd hidden himself somewhere, and was waiting for a new summons that would bring him around. This didn't happen. I pounded against the glass, I resumed yelling but this time more enticingly: Mario, come here, I've thought of a great game. And it was true, I wanted to send him to look for my cell phone. With the cell everything would be easier: I could show him the symbol for previously made calls, then his mother's name, and once we called Betta she could get in touch with Sally and send her to me. But in reply the house merely resounded with cartoon voices, loathsome and shrill, at top volume. I called out hoarsely—Mario, Mario, Mario—in vain: It was obvious he didn't want to hear me. On the other hand, even if he had heard me, even if he came back to the balcony, where had I left my cell phone?

I struggled to remember, and when I did, I grew even more depressed. The phone was right in front of me, a few yards beyond the double-paned glass. I'd placed it on one of the highest shelves, in the midst of knickknacks that had belonged to a teenaged Betta, and I'd done it so as to prevent Mario from being able to reach it. In fact he'd never be able to get at it, not even standing up on a chair. But even were he able to, it wouldn't have done any good. In the same instant I remembered that I hadn't charged it in at least three days. The cell was no doubt as useless as the cordless.

What stupid lack of foresight, I only cared about the inessential. I was still crouched against the glass, I was afraid even to stand. I was like those people who hate flying and spend the whole time never going to the bathroom, never even crossing their legs, terrified that if they simply leave their spot the plane will tilt, wobble, flip over, and plummet to a crash. On the other hand I had to come up with something, shout, seek—let's see—to attract the attention of neighbors, of passersby. But how? I was on the sixth floor, peripheral to all that was happening on the street, overwhelmed by the noise. Never mind the fact that, if no one noticed the screaming voices from the cartoons, who would register my own cries, choked by the cold? I sighed, I was cooking up excuses and I knew it. What really prevented me from waving my arms and calling out for help was shame. I'd wanted to be *more* than the place I'd grown up in, I'd sought out the world's approval. And now that I was at the end of my life and taking stock of it, I couldn't bear looking like a hysterical little man who screamed for help from the balcony of the old house in which he'd been a young boy, the one he'd fled from, full of ambition. I was ashamed of being locked outside, I was ashamed that I hadn't known how to avoid it, I was ashamed to find myself lacking the controlled haughtiness that had always prevented me from asking anyone for help, I was ashamed of being an old man imprisoned by a child.

This child, right: Who could guarantee that he really was sitting in an armchair in front of the TV? Maybe he was roaming through the house, prey to all the words his parents had imprudently instilled in him. He could have turned on the gas. He could have lit a fire, set himself on fire. He could have turned on the faucets and flooded everything. He could have drowned in the bathtub or slashed himself with his father's razor blades. He could have climbed up onto the furniture and, pulling it down on himself, been crushed. My imagination started to multiply the dangers, and the more my distress for Mario's fate mounted, the more he—thanks to an incongruous slippage—seemed my enemy, an enemy who was already an adult, already powerful. I recalled the look he'd thrown me when he'd said, I'm going to watch cartoons. I'd never had that sort of strength, the strength to say: Either do what I say or pay the price. I'd been, as far as I could remember, a child in the woodwork. Sure, I'd often harbored dark, nasty feelings, but I'd always embarked on oblique paths to express them. Mario, on the other hand, possessed the chromosomes of someone who confronts whoever stands in his way, and wins. Or, who knows, now I was exaggerating, he was just like any kid and he was behaving like a kid. I was the problem, I who'd squandered my vitality so that now just sensing the energy in this tiny body exasperated me. He'd even managed to devalue my artistic skills, I thought. He'd shown that he could learn from me, in no time, all the little things I knew how to do. He'd shown me that he could do them better, immediately, now, at the age of four. And he did all this so that I intuited what he would be able to do in the future, once he'd stopped growing, when—in the event that he embarked on my same path, scaling down the thousands of other possibilities open to ferocious beasts like him—he'd erase me with his bravura, he'd cancel every memory of my work, he'd reduce me to a relative with a feeble creative vocation, to a clump of time spent in mediocrity.

I decided to stand up again; I had to find a solution. I cast a cautious glance down below, holding myself firmly against the railing. Some lights were on now. I couldn't see well but it looked like the first floor was illuminated, a glow spreading through the darkness of the courtyard. Maybe, I thought, I can count on the enmity of Attilio's mother. I thought about

provoking her, lowering the bucket with toys. I considered tor-
menting her and her husband by dangling the receptacle in
front of their glass door. Feeling stupid, I did just that—a guy
over seventy playing like a little boy. I made sure the bucket
was dangling at the height of the first floor and I convinced
myself, give or take an inch, that it was. With my left hand I
held myself against the railing, and with the right I imparted a
wavering movement to the cord, hoping that someone would
appear, cursing, in the patch of light. Nothing. Desolate, I let
the bucket dangle for a while. I heard the blood pounding in
my head. Still holding myself steady with my left hand, I
tugged the cord a bit, then let go of it abruptly, various times.
Nothing, still nothing. So I pulled up the bucket, angrily; I did
it in no time, it was light. I wanted to throw the toys down, try
to hit the balcony. But when the bucket was within arm's reach,
I saw that it was empty.

3.

I was heartened; someone in those few minutes had taken
the toys. Had it been Attilio? His mother? The father?
Whichever one of them had done it, it would have triggered a
reaction. The woman, above all, would feel insulted, she'd run
up here in a rage to ring the bell. Ah, god bless rage. Now I just
had to figure out a way to get Mario to turn off the television,
or at the very least, lower the volume. We both ran the risk of
not hearing the bell.

I went back to the glass door, still holding the bucket. I
started pounding with my free palm, shouting: Mario, come
back to Grandpa, I have something amazing to tell you. My
temples were throbbing, my throat hurt, I was freezing. I
ended up changing my tone of voice almost without wanting
to: Mario, what are you doing, don't make me get angry, come

back here, now. And while I was hollering, increasingly out of control, perhaps due to the effort, perhaps due to the hemoglobin and ferritin, there appeared before me, beyond the double-paned glass, a repugnant spectacle. The opposite wall, the one my bed was pushed up against, was an enormous piece of lard pocked with thin reddish strips, and numerous evil faces were protruding from the fat.

I closed my eyes, I opened them again. The lard was still there, thick with tiny living faces, overwhelming me with nausea. Aghast, I tried to get rid of the hallucination with other images, but I only managed to replace it with one that seemed immediately more threatening. I saw the main door that Mario would have to run to if one of the tenants from the first floor were to ring the bell. The vision was hyperrealistic, I pictured the brown sections of the door, the dark iron of the armor plating, the handle, the knob of the bolt. And I realized that even if the whole family had come: father, mother, Attilio, his brothers; even if they rang the bell with furious persistence; even if I were able to comunicate with Mario and send him to the door, the child would never be capable of opening it, because I myself had closed up from the inside, to keep him from going back down to his friend's place. Mario could only reach the brass knob of the bolt by climbing a ladder. But he'd never be able to carry it out of the closet, open it, set it down properly. And even if he were able to, what good would it do? The child's hands wouldn't be strong enough to make the two turns of the knob necessary to open up.

An endless moment passed. I'm worn out, I thought, I'm cold, it's about to rain, I don't want to die on this little balcony that I hate, it's time to break something. And since I could think of no reason not to, I shifted the bucket to my right hand and struck the glass with whatever strength I had left. I expected the door to be reduced to a thousand shards, I tried to keep my distance so I wouldn't get hurt. But the bucket sounded like a rubber ball against an obstacle and bounced back without damaging anything. I lost my wits and started to strike doggedly, one strike after the next, accompanied by shouts that seemed to rend my throat. Since this had no effect on the glass, I stopped, worn out completely. My wrist hurt and I rubbed it. Nonetheless I was about to proceed to kicks, but I remembered just in time that I was wearing slippers. I would have broken my bones while doing no damage to the glass door. I gave up.

How fragile I'd become. If, once, I used to believe in each of my gestures, if I used to think that merely a well-conceived stroke of my pencil could split a mountain in two, now even glass overwhelmed me. I saw myself reflected, bucket in hand, knees apart, bent forward, face with deep hollows beneath the ridge of my brows, the broad curve of cheekbones above my withered face. Thus, in the wind, crushed by the blackness of the sky, my nerves wounded by the clamorous street, numbed to the bone, I suddenly felt comical. Here was a seventy-five-year-old man, slovenly, disheveled, pants falling down: He should be minding a child and instead he's incapable of minding himself. I thought back to Mario's idea of pulling up the emptiness with the bucket and it made me laugh. Maybe it really was the only way out of this situation: Lower the bucket once, twice, thrice, a thousand times, cancel the abyss, climb over the railing and look for help. You had to work patiently, diligently: one bucketful after another of all the emptiness that had terrified my mother, and now frightened me. That way the balcony would be nothing other than a sliver of narrow stone wedged between the double-paned glass of the apartment, the glass facade of the station, the windows of the cars and of the houses opposite, firmly contained inside a well-devised whole. The kid had a good eye. What was he, what would he become when he grew up? I, as a young boy, had proudly felt like the crucible of the most varied expectations of my mother. She lit up with pride when the teacher would tell her: This child is exceptional, he'll do great things as an adult. She'd come home fortified by the school's authoritative words. She believed. No one could recall anyone in our family who had done great things. Not even among our friends, acquaintances, and neighbors. Those who did great things were rare figures, you didn't meet them, you couldn't talk to them or touch them. I was the only exceptional one, the teacher had assured my mother. And she would tell my father, tell anyone, something that made me incredibly happy. That sentence filled me to the brim, it had filled me my whole life, despite my many doubts. Really, what were great things? What distinguished them from small ones? Where was the authority that established whether things were great or small? And then, with the passing years, the competition had grown tenfold. As long as those of us who aspired to great things were few, believing in our extraordinary nature had been an utterly private act of faith. Feeling unique had come easily, and proving it, well, all it had taken was a little success, a bit of presumption, manifesting some sign of depression or madness that squared well with clichés about talent. Over time, however, exceptionalism had spread. Forty years ago the cream of the crop had already started to press, in large numbers, against the factories of art and culture, against their narrow doors. To an extent that now—I would often say, grousing alone in my house in Milan—being exceptional had become the desperate cry of the masses along the infinite routes of television and the Internet, a widespread excellence, badly paid, often unemployed. I'd been thinking this way for some years, confusedly, and at times those thoughts depressed me. What, in the end, had I been? Had I merely been part of an avant-garde that had opened the floodgates to today's throng of creatives? Had I been among the unheralded who, more than half a century ago, had inaugurated an ever-growing illusion of greatness? Come to think of it, I'd gotten old with the conviction that, sooner or later, some incredible event would banish my doubts forever, thereby defining me with extreme precision. The event I'd always awaited was that some work of mine, undeniably huge, bursting into the world, would prove that I wasn't presumptuous. Now that all-clarifying event had arrived, and what's more, in my city of origin. It had nothing to do with one of my works, it had to do with that ridiculous prison on the balcony of my early adolescence. Mario, a petulant child, had been the instigator; he'd wanted to pretend to be an artist with his grandfather; in a heartbeat, performing a trick, he'd stripped the fullness induced by the now distant praise of teachers and professors from my body. To play a trick, he'd locked me outside. As I stood there, exposed to the icy wind and the rain that threatened to fall, the truth seemed obvious to me at last. My body hadn't been depleted of energy only in recent months because of surgery. My body had always been empty, ever since adolescence, ever since childhood, ever since my birth. I'd been wrong about myself, thanks to my stubbornness I'd become something I wasn't suited to being. Certainly, I'd worked hard and I'd been lucky. Discreet consensus and conspicuous success had been soldered to childhood praise. But there was no way out, I had no virtues, I was empty. The precipice wasn't on the other side of the railing, the precipice was within me. And this was something I couldn't bear. I'd lower the bucket down my throat just to pull out that emptiness.

I touched my forehead: drops of rain. I angrily tossed the bucket over the railing, I threw myself against the door, I yelled through it. Mario, I called with whatever voice I had left, and to my surprise I felt myself echo so loudly that I froze, straining to listen. The music and shrill voices and silly sounds of cartoon animals had ceased. The child must have finally turned off the television.

4.

I waited on tenterhooks. Mario appeared, content, the look of some cartoon character still in his eyes.

—He, he said, amused, he followed him, Grandpa, and he ended up banging against a tree.

I didn't ask who *he* was, afraid that he would start explaining it to me.

—Did it make you laugh?

—Yes.

—Good. Now can you do something for me?

—Right away.

—Can you try to turn this handle the way your father does when the door's blocked?

—I need to get a chair.

—Don't bother, you can manage without it.

—But to do a good job I need to be as tall as Dad.

He didn't wait for me to give him permission, he went to one of the chairs in the room and pushed it up to the glass door.

—Be careful.

—I'm being good.

He climbed on top of the chair while I was saying to myself, trepidatiously: If he falls and hurts himself, what will I do? But he didn't fall. Standing up straight, he grasped the handle.

—You have to force it.

—I know.

Lips straight, eyes focused, he moved the handle up and down, then shouted out enthusiastically: Done! I pushed the door cautiously. He hadn't done a damn thing, the door was closed.

—Bravo. Want to try again?

—I opened it.

—Mario, it's not a game, try again. The door really has to open.

He avoided my gaze, staring at the floor.

—I'm hungry.

—Will you please try again for me?

—I'm hungry, Grandpa.

It had started to rain. My ears and neck were freezing. I said:

—If you want to eat then you need to let me back into the house. Try again.

He whined:

—I haven't even had a snack, I'm going to tell Mom.

—The handle, Mario.

—No, he said, getting angry. I'm hungry. And without warning he jumped down from the chair, and I felt my heart in my throat.

—You OK? I asked.

He stood up again.

—I can jump better than anyone, at nursery school.

Who knows how many things he thought he did better than anyone. And who knows how much time he'd spend thinning the number of those primates, whittling them down to one or two, only to conclude that not a single one of them really sparkled. I said:

—Sure you didn't hurt yourself? Why are your rubbing your ankle?

—It hurts a tiny bit right here. I'm going to get something to eat, that way it'll go away.

—Mario, I called out, while he, pretending to limp, prepared to vanish once again.

—Wait, I'm hungry, too.

—I'll bring you some bread.

—Don't you dare cut the bread with a knife, I shouted when he'd already turned down the hallway.

But was that prohibition alone enough? How many more things should I have forbidden him to do? Make himself a sandwich. Prepare a frittata. Use the microwave to thaw Sally's food. And so much more. He had the whole apartment to stage, with verisimilitude, his performance as omniscient homunculus. Saverio had trained him to do too many things inappropriate for a four-year-old and he protected himself by playing. He could convince himself that he could do everything only because the game allowed him to hide his failures. He was so good at miming competence, he took credit with such aplomb. I remembered that, long ago, people used to speak to kids in kid lingo. It was a crazy language but it demarcated a certain distance; pushing little kids toward adult verbalization, only to flaunt their great intelligence, didn't exist yet. My wife and I had been among those in our generation who'd gotten rid of words like boo-boo. Betta spoke like a book when she was three, maybe even more than her son. We'd been so proud of her, we'd shown her off, asking questions the way you ask a parrot. The result? An outsized childhood, followed by the frustration of never being able to give as much as she felt entitled to give. Which is perhaps why she said to Mario: I'll give you a *tottò* on your hands.

A *tottò*, to be honest, was something I'd have gladly given him myself at that point. I was about to hurl another cry in the child's direction—and meanwhile I shielded my hair with a hand, the humidity must have been affecting my hearing, I must have had a headache, an earache, a neck ache, a fever—when I thought I heard a loud ringing. I waited with bated breath. Had the people on the first floor found the toys, had Attilio's mother decided to make a punishing delivery? I focused, trying to block out the traffic noises. Yes, there was the loud ringing again, unequivocal. I pounded against the glass, Mario, Mario, Mario. This time the child rushed back:

—The doorbell, Grandpa. It's Mom.

—It's not Mom. Can you please pay attention to what I tell you?

—It's Mom, I'm going to open up.

—You can't open up, Mario, just listen to me: Now go run to the door and say, as loud as you can, these very words: My grandfather's locked out on the balcony, call for help. Repeat after me.

Mario shook his head.

—I know how to open to door, I can do it, it's Mom.

I said, forcing myself to sound calm:

—Mario, I'm telling you, it's not Mom and you can't open the door, it's bolted shut. Go repeat the words I'm saying: My grandfather's locked out on the balcony, call for help.

Again the bell rang loudly, frantically. Mario couldn't resist, he shouted: Coming, and took off.

I stood there waiting, the rain was getting harder. There was so much traffic that, no matter how hard I listened, I barely heard a thing. I figured the child would attempt nevertheless to open the door. I figured he'd drag a chair up to the door to try to reach the brass knob. He was a stubborn creature, I doubted he'd immediately say what I'd ask him. But I hoped that, in the end, given how housebroken he was, he'd utter the sentence, just for the pleasure of pronouncing it. I paid attention to every minute sound, and in spite of the thunder I heard the bell ring again. Whoever was waiting on the landing, they'd be aware of Mario behind the door. I ruled out that the child would have remained silent. Maybe he wouldn't say exactly what I'd told him, but surely he'd have yelled out something. I counted on it, and meanwhile the stress was eating me alive. No more loud ringing. Had the person from the first floor stopped, were they talking now?

Mario turned up again in the room.

—It wasn't Mom, he said.

—Who was it?

—I opened up and there was nobody.

—Tell me the truth, Mario. Did you really open the door?

He was looking at the floor, he was upset.

—I'm going to get something to eat.

—Wait, answer me: did you really open the door or are you pretending?

—I have a huge stomachache, Grandpa, and now I'm really hungry.

—Remember what you were supposed to say: My grandfather's on the balcony, he can't get in? Did you say it?

—Ugh, I don't want to play anymore, I'm hungry.

5.

He went away, dejected. I'd gotten myself into a mess, I was sick of everything, of the child most of all. It was his fault that I was standing in the rain, which was now falling hard. I turned my back on the room, I hated that apartment, I tried to stick my shoulders as much as possible to the glass so that I wouldn't get wet. The water was mixed with wind, wailing gusts, the stuff of Gothic novels, and the drops embroidered my shadow, extending on the balcony, with shifting, sparkling threads. No, there was no shelter to be had. The rain struck me forcefully, drenching my pants, my slippers, my pullover. Roaring sheets of water descended from the cornice, the sky flashed continuously, and the thunder was endless. Futile car-alarm concerts rose up from the instantly flooded street. But above all it was the dark of the courtyard, of the great public square, that seemed to swallow up most of the water. From that gloom rose a gelid whirl, as if the illuminated balcony were a bridge suspended over an eddying torrent.

This terrified me, and I turned around to look into the room, to see if Mario had come back. Had he fallen off the chair after he'd tried to turn the knob, was that why he was in such a bad mood? Had he gone back to the kitchen, forgetting about me, consumed by his need to eat? And what, in the kitchen, was he doing? What if the lights went out in the neighborhood, and the whole house went dark, and the child had to manage on his own? And I, even more alone, in the rain? My teeth were chattering nonstop, it was as if I could no longer breathe. Water dripped from my soaked hair into my eyes, down my neck, into my ears, and anguish coursed through my heart. The images that I myself had conceived in the past few days came back to haunt me: The old house juxtaposed itself upon the new; the sketches leapt off the pages creating waves of former possibilities and probabilities; the ghosts broke all barriers—so many I's, either aborted or short-lived—and they scurried through the house, seeking me out. What a lame outcome. Soon my neck started to hurt, accompanied by vertigo, nausea. And along with the nausea, the enormous piece of streaked lard: repulsive primogenital matter. But little faces trying to free themselves no longer protruded from it. Instead, Mario was buried in the lard, his small form gathered up and ready to spill out, slick with fat. It was useless closing my eyes, useless opening them again, the form didn't go away. This is what I need to draw, I thought. Mario was the ghost I was looking for, he'd been right under my nose ever since I'd arrived. His living matter itself contains all possibility: what's manifested though the long chain of couplings and births that came before him, what's undone and lost in death, what waits a thousand years to manifest itself and now twists, squirms, distends, demanding a present tense in the future, wanting to be drawn, painted, photographed, filmed, downloaded, broadcast, recounted, reconsidered. What an astonishing ghost that child was, so small, so able. I couldn't stand him, I couldn't stand anything anymore. I felt violent gusts of rain on my shoulders. The water's cold surge—I imagined—must have reached the little balcony, transforming it into a resplendent raft above the black mold of the liquefied city. Until the thunder crashed so that all of Naples shook.

Mario burst quickly into the room, a piece of bread in each hand, yelling:

—Grandpa, I'm scared.

I have to get him to stay here, I thought. I have to treat him right, he's all I've got.

—There's nothing to be scared of, I said, forcing myself not to shudder from the cold. Thunder is just a noise, like car horns, hear them?

—You're all wet.

—It's raining.

—I want to get wet, too.

—As soon as you open this door.

—I will, after I eat my bread.

—Okay.

He climbed back onto the chair, helping himself up with his chest and elbows, then stood up. He took a big bite out of one of the pieces of bread, and held the other one out to me.

—This one's yours, he said. Eat.

He pressed it against the glass. I opened my mouth wide, I chewed at the air. I muttered:

—Yummy, so yummy, thank you.

—Why are you talking like that?

—Because I'm terribly cold. Hear the wind, see how it's raining?

The child studied me attentively.

—Are you sick?

—A little, I'm old. The cold and the rain can make me sick.

—And die?

—Yes.

—When will you die?

—Soon.

—My dad says when mean people die you don't have to be sorry.

—I'm not mean, I'm distracted.

—Even though you're distracted I'll cry when you die.

—No, your dad said you don't need to feel sorry.

—I'll still cry.

In the meantime he devoured his bread, never forgetting to ask me to eat mine. Only when he'd finished did I come to a decision. I told him: Mario, you're an extraordinary child, so try to understand what I'm saying. Until now we've had a good time. You tricked me by locking me outside, we've talked on the phone, we've eaten. But now all the games are over. Grandpa really feels very faint. I'm so cold that I need to warm up right away, if not I'll die, not pretend but for real. Look how hard it's raining, have you seen the lightning, heard the thunder? So much water's pouring down, it feels like this balcony's in the middle of the ocean. I'm scared. I'm seeing and hearing terrible things, I'm on the verge of crying. In this moment I'm no longer the grown-up, I'm younger than you. Actually, I should tell you the truth: Now you're the grown-up, only you. You're stronger, you're smarter, and you need to save me. Eat up my piece of bread, too, that way you'll be even stronger. And then think hard and try to remember how you unlock the door, you need to do exactly what your father does. You can do it, you know how, you know everything at your age, you can do it. Are you listening to me, Mario? Do you realize the mess you've gotten me into? Do you realize that if I die out here it's your fault? Do you know what'll happen to you when your mother gets back? Come on, hurry up, we're not playing anymore. Concentrate, and turn this fucking handle the right way.

I'd started off right. I'd set out with the intention of making a final attempt. I wanted to convey, to the child, an idea of reality, of responsibility, of utmost duty. But by now I'd almost entirely lost track of those sentiments, and the affectionate voice had turned increasingly aggressive without my wanting it to. And so I'd botched the finale, panic combined with fury had overwhelmed me. *Are you listening to me, Mario? Do you realize the mess you've gotten me into? Do you realize that if I die out here it's your fault? Do you know what'll happen to you when your mother gets back? Come on, hurry up, we're not playing anymore. Concentrate, and turn this fucking handle the right way.* At that moment something ruptured, and out came all the aversion I'd felt toward him ever since the day I'd arrived, since he'd told me the drawings were dark. I shouted in dialect, I pounded the glass, forgetting, this time, that it might make things worse, injuring me and injuring him.

What brought me to that point? I don't know. Certainly, in striking the glass, I wanted to strike him, but not the determined child standing on the chair—no, surely not—but rather the form made of lard that had flashed before me, the concentrate of amorphous power that I now saw in him, all the repugnant living substance that continuously blows up in your face like buboes, that becomes language, that shapes and reshapes each and every thing, that cuts and pastes always tricking itself, always disappointed. When I threw the last punch I must have looked like the ghastliest of hell's bloodsucking shades. Mario, whose eyes were already filled with tears, shuddered, drew back, and fell off the chair.

6.

The fear of what might have happened to the child suddenly stunned me in my tracks. I gave up on smashing the double-paned glass with bare hands, I was being lashed by the rain, my right hand still raised. Where was Mario, was he hurt? The water was blinding me, I could only hear him screaming. Mario, I called out, did you hurt yourself? Don't cry, answer me. He was on the ground beside the chair. He was lying on his back, he was moving his arms, kicking and crying the way disconsolate children cry, heedlessly, hurling out desperate wails. He was small, exposed to everything. I'd never managed to see him, over the past few days, in such a defenseless, speechless state, without those knowing glances of his. All of his movements were out of control and the tears weren't aimed at getting something or complaining about something else, they were tears of bewilderment, of collapse. The kind of tears he'd harbored for who knows how long behind his *I know, I'll do it*, seeking the approval of an incomprehensible grandfather who'd always been the enemy.

—Mario, listen, come here.

—No, he screamed, even louder, chasing away my voice by frenetically striking the air. He cried and cried, I was terrified, he was so distraught that he seemed prey to convulsions. Then little by little he calmed down, the desperation was ebbing. I said:

—Get up, let's see what's happened to you.

—No.

—Did you bang your head?

—No.

—Does it hurt somewhere?

—Yes.

—Where?

—I don't know.

—Come here and I'll give you a kiss where it hurts.

—No, you're the one who made me fall.

—I didn't do it on purpose.

—I'm telling Mommy.

—Okay but come get a kiss, kisses make you better.

—Kisses don't matter, you need ointments.

—Kisses matter, want to make a bet?

He picked himself up, flushed, tears and snot dripping down his face, his lips shiny with spit, shaken by sobs that were fainter now. Every step of the way I thought he was dragging strips of the room behind him: whitish filaments of the greasy wall, proteins and enzymes. In that living action figure I believed there was something—also—that for the past seventy years had seemed only mine and that came, instead, from a very distant place. It had traveled from one segment of flesh-bone-nerves-time to another analogous segment, amid ferocious ruptures and starts, disappearing, reappearing. Who knew how many, marveling at themselves, had traced ambitious marks on water or dust, and joined flashing stars at night, or sketched lively adventures along random lines in the rocks, up the corrugations of bark, or even thumbing through cards with fingertips that altered fate, fair or foul may it be. Ghosts make their nests in the future. Now Mario, the goblin in him invincible, was touching his right knee, he was doing this insistently, reenacting the damage I'd caused. He drew his knee up to the glass, I bent down to kiss it, and since I still wasn't at the same height as the hurt leg, I kneeled down in the water, curving over, and kissed the glass door, wetting my lips with the ice-cold rain running in rivulets over them.

—How is it? I asked.

—A little OK.

—See how kisses help?

—Yeah.

—Who's Grandpa's angel?

—Me.

—Move your leg, let me see if it hurts.

He moved it energetically.

—It doesn't hurt anymore.

—Now sit and I'll tell you a fairy tale.

—No, you're cold and shivering. Now I'll give you a kiss so you feel better.

He gave it to the glass.

—Feel better?

—Much better.

—Now I'll go get the screwdriver and open the door for you.

I was scared that he was going away again. I said, sincerely supplicating:

—Stay here, keep me company.

—I'll be right back.

—Please, don't do anything dangerous. Come, let's play with your toys, Grandpa doesn't want to be by himself.

Impossible, he was quivering with excitement, there was no holding him back. He'd suddenly returned to the realm he liked best, the one where he could pull off anything. I tried to find the strength to stand up again. The rain was tapering off, soon it would cease. I'd been reduced to such a state: soaked through, from my head down to my slippers, exposed to the wind that continued to blow. The disaster now struck me as so extreme that I found it amusing. Something had happened in the past few minutes that I was only beginning to absorb, and which to my surprise was calming me down. I must have crossed a barrier without realizing it, and now I could no longer worry about myself. Life, my whole life, had slipped to the side, it was behind me, no regrets. I wouldn't illustrate James, it was beyond me, and in any case I no longer had the energy to try again. What I knew how to do was limited, it was useless trying to accomplish more. Mario's drawing, on the other hand, yes, that was *more*. Nice lines, who knew if they would ever yield fruit. And this yielding of fruit, such an obsession. Since adolescence I'd attributed too much importance to it, and instead—it was clear to me now—in the end it was nothing other than drawing, coloring, an idle pleasure. I could have devoted myself to truer things, at first I'd had the urge: changing, adjusting, mitigating, and teaching people to change, adjust, mitigate. Instead I'd played into my old age in order to pass the time. I'd wanted to keep the horror that spread through the house, through the street, on the face of the earth, at a distance, filtering in everything that, around it, seemed peaceful, sacred, devout. Instead it stretched, it spilt at the seams, it suffered, breaking into shards. Thank goodness Mario was coming back. A tinny scraping sound in the hallway announced his presence, and then he appeared, pushing a metal box through the room, up to the glass door. He was purple from the strain, again he'd surely risked hurting himself in order to move that heavy object. I told him he didn't have to bring the whole toolbox, that he could have just brought the screwdriver since it was the only thing he needed. That's what Dad does, he replied, and he sat on the ground, capably opened the box, and pulled out a screwdriver with a yellow handle.

—Don't get on the chair, I warned.

—I'm not, I need to stick the screwdriver into a little hole down here.

—Fine, play with it, but don't scratch the door, it's new.

—I'm not playing, Grandpa, I'm really doing it.

—I'm happy for you. It's nice playing at doing things for real.

He remained seated on the floor but dragged his rear end up to the door. I, standing, kept my eyes on him, if only to affix them to something steady and bright. In truth, in part because of my position, in part because of my wet lenses, in part because the glass door in between was cloudy with condensation, in part because I felt that my strength really was about to give way, I couldn't see a thing, and only hoped, calmly however, that Mario wouldn't hurt himself with the screwdriver.

—Did you say abracadabra?

—Dad doesn't say it.

—Tricks work better with abracadabra.

—Abracadabra.

—Well then?

He abandoned his instrument on the floor, stood up, and soberly said:

—Done.

—Bravo, I said softly, and it occurred to me that we live our whole lives as if the ceaseless measuring of things and ourselves related to some indisputable truth; then, in old age, we realize that it's only a matter of conventions, each of them inter-changeable at any moment with others, and that the key thing is to trust the ones that seem to us, time after time, most reas-suring. My grandson stood up, looking quite satisfied. He put the screwdriver back into the toolbox, as usual following Saverio's directions, and the rules for tidiness imposed by his mother. Then he turned back to me. With both hands he low-ered the handle and the glass door opened.

7.

I stepped inside, immediately shutting the door behind me, afraid that the balcony would pull me back out. I fêted the child without touching him, I was too wet. You can do every-thing, I told him, what multitudes you contain, you're amazing. Then straightaway I turned on the shower, I threw off my drenched clothes and slipped under the boiling stream of water still wearing my socks and underwear. Mario found this thrilling, he wanted to do the same thing, and I let him.

—I'm keeping my socks and underwear on, too.

—Okay.

The heat restored my soul, spirit, the breath of life. The electrochemical reactions, whatever they are. Nothing, how-ever, compared with what exploded in sharp cries and laugh-ter from the child's body for the whole time we danced under the water, the whole time we spent in our bathrobes, me pressed right up against the bathroom radiator, him dodging the hair dryer's blast.

—You're burning me.

—Don't be ridiculous.

—You don't know how to do it, your hair doesn't get dry that way.

—You're right, Grandpa's an old fool, but it's over now, we're done.

We thawed the last of Sally's meals, we ate, we got into our pajamas, we watched cartoons until the child passed out. I put him to bed and was about to lie down myself—I was worn out, my eyelids were closing—but first I wanted to charge the cordless and the cell phone, then see if the glass door really did have, at the bottom, a little miraculous hole. I didn't find one, but if truth be told my eyesight left much to be desired. As soon as my head hit the pillow I fell asleep.

Sally woke us up the next day. Sleepyhead Grandpa, sleepyhead Grandson, she said, pulling up the blind. Then she showed the child, still incredibly drowsy, two action figures and a car: She wanted to know why he'd left them on the landing. Then she moved on to me, speaking at the top of her voice: I've never seen this house in such a mess, what did you do, did you play with water? I said nothing, I only asked: Would you step outside, please? The child meanwhile hollered out: I want to go back to sleep, don't touch my toys.

Sally fixed us breakfast. We discovered that she was in a fine mood, she'd just gotten engaged to a waiter from Scafati. She told us that the waiter was shy, he was three years older, a widower with four grown children. She'd given herself the day off because he tarried in expressing his love and she needed to give him a shove. She asked me:

—You have a girlfriend, Grandpa?

—No.

—I have lots, Mario said, though he was speaking to me.

—I have no doubt, I replied. Grandpa on the other hand never had much luck with girlfriends.

—If you want I can give you one of mine, the child offered.

—I wanted me and Mario to go steady, Sally interrupted, but he didn't love me and said no.

—You're old, the child said.

—So's Grandpa.

—Not my Grandpa.

The entire time I was shaving Mario wanted to stand next to me. At a certain point he said:

—Maybe Mom and Dad will get divorced.

I was happy he'd decided to confide in me this way.

—Do you know what divorce means?

—Yes.

—I don't believe you, explain it.

—It means they'll leave me.

—See how you didn't know? They leave each other, but they don't leave you.

He said nothing, embarrassed, then said:

—If they get divorced can I come to your house?

—For as long as you want.

He looked relieved. He asked:

—Are you going to work today?

—No, I'm not going to work anymore.

—Really?

—Really.

—Dad says, He who doesn't work doesn't eat.

—Your dad's always right, I won't eat.

—If you don't work, can we play?

—No, it's sunny today, let's go out.

—I'm not walking, though.

—Me neither. We'll take the subway.

He was overjoyed. For him—I discovered—the subway was a kind of Disneyland. The thing he liked most was the escalator at Piazza Garibaldi, but that wasn't enough to satisfy him, he intended to visit every station. Let's go down, look around a little, then come back up—he said, mapping our itinerary—

Dad and I do it sometimes. I agreed, and we spent most of our time at Toledo Station. We went up and down the escalators, he wanted to show me the effects of the colors and lights on the walls. He explained: That's the sun, Grandpa, and here's the sea, and here you can see San Gennaro and Vesuvius. The morning flew by, as did the rest of the day. In the evening, Betta called. She seemed happy, at first I didn't understand why. Then it emerged that she was feeling proud of Saverio, his presentation had been generously received, by now people at the convention spoke of nothing else. And the rest of it? I asked. She replied, just great, and she wanted to say hi to her son. I handed him the cordless but kept listening. Mario recounted our exploration of the subway in minute detail to his mother, and told her about Sally's engagement. He mentioned nothing about the balcony.

Indeed, he and I hadn't talked about the balcony either, not for the whole day. At a certain point, as I was sneezing and coughing—I was coming down with a bad cold—he'd asked with concern: Did you throw off the covers last night, Grandpa? That was it.

Maybe that whole business had had little effect on him. Or, more likely, in his warehouse of adult expressions to unsheathe at the right moment, he hadn't found one for the balcony, and so he'd shelved it in a place beyond words, for god knows how long. At night, he only reminded me, if you throw off the covers, you'll catch cold.

8.

The next day his parents returned, arriving at around three in the afternoon. I noted that, though he worshipped his father, he threw himself into his mother's arms. She picked him up, smothering him at length with kisses.

—Happy I'm back?

—Yes.

—How'd it go with Grandpa?

—Really great.

—Did you let him work?

—He doesn't work anymore.

That news didn't upset my daughter in the least. She reacted by saying: He doesn't work anymore because you're impossible, god knows how much you tortured him. And she laughed. She's always had beautiful teeth, just like Ada's. The laughter lit up her face, her whole body, and it revealed to me that she'd changed, it was as if she'd just been woken from a night of pleasant dreams that seemed true. Come to Mommy, she said to the child, and she didn't let go of him all afternoon.

I spent my time with Saverio; he bored me, but what could I do about it? I told him, I heard you were a huge success in Cagilari. He acknowledged this with a nod of false modesty, but he wasn't able to contain himself for very long, and though he knew that I understood nothing about mathematics he explained to me, in minute detail, the cutting-edge content of his talk. I felt the little energy I had draining away, I was sneezing a lot and coughing. You're brilliant in your field, I tossed out, if only to interrupt him. He replied in his typically formal way: And you're so brilliant in yours. I played it down and, since I didn't know what else to say, asked about him and Betta.

It was a mistake, he turned red, a redness so obvious that I tried to look away so as not to embarrass him. I did and said some stupid things, he admitted reluctantly. His breathing was shallow and he was now gesticulating, now clasping his hands together as if he never wanted them to part. He made me a list of his obsessions, the waking nightmares he'd had. And he apologized to me, he wanted me to pardon him for what he'd said about my daughter.

—Insane stuff, he murmured, his eyes bright. She loves me, she always has, and in exchange I torment her.

His regret was sincere. I was happy that he contributed to my grandson's genome and I told him so, with obvious irony. But Saverio took it seriously, he thanked me, and he went on to blather about the analysis he'd been in for years, never ridding himself of those harrowing fantasies.

—What should I do? he asked me.

—Everything, I muttered. A pinch of drugs, a touch of sociology, a smidge of psychology, a smear of religion. A bit of revolt and revolution, a drop of art. Maybe even a vegetarian diet, an English class, Astronomy. It depends on the seasons.

—What seasons?

—The seasons of life.

He shook his head, as if he wanted to throw it off his neck.

—You're joking, but I'm flawed. Jealousy is a gene that makes me see what's not there.

I felt like smiling. I confessed that in my case things had gone differently:

—I don't have that gene, and I ended up not seeing what was there. But now that I'm looking harder, I'm seeing huge chunks of lard streaked with lean meat everywhere.

—Is it a new painting you're thinking of making?

—No, it's reality.

—You're funny. I can never make people laugh.

—Me neither, but today I'm in a good mood so things are a bit better.

—Did you finish your illustrations?

—No.

—Because you're a perfectionist. I've always thought we were sort of alike, maybe that's why your daughter wanted to be with me.

—You think so?

—Sure. I take people where they can never go with an

equation, and you do the same thing with a stroke of your brush.

I'd never taken anyone anywhere, but I didn't want to disappoint him. We chatted for quite a while with startling ease, until Mario turned up again. He leaned against one of his father's legs and asked:

—So what did you and Grandpa get up to?

Mario grimaced, squirming, looking up and looking down—he was pretending to think—then said, pointing at me happily:

—He went out on the balcony and we played.

—In this cold?

—Grandpa was the one on the balcony, not me.

—Ah, got it. And you had a good time?

—Super good.

Betta also poked her head in. It seemed that nothing could upset her, not me, not her husband, not her son. Things must have been rough in recent months, but now she was prepared to fight tooth and nail for her well-being, to defend it with lies. She was holding a sheet of paper in her hands. It was Mario's drawing, the one that had so upset me.

—Dad, she said, with a note of irony in her voice, what's this? A fresh start, regained youth? It's lovely.

She'd never wasted words in praise of the things I'd done. Rather—I recalled—she'd been quite critical as an adolescent, almost offensive, then after twenty she limited herself to the indulgence of a daughter who'd come to accept her father's fatuity.

—My grandson did it, I said proudly.

But Mario shouted out, practically at the same time:

—I copied Grandpa.

APPENDIX

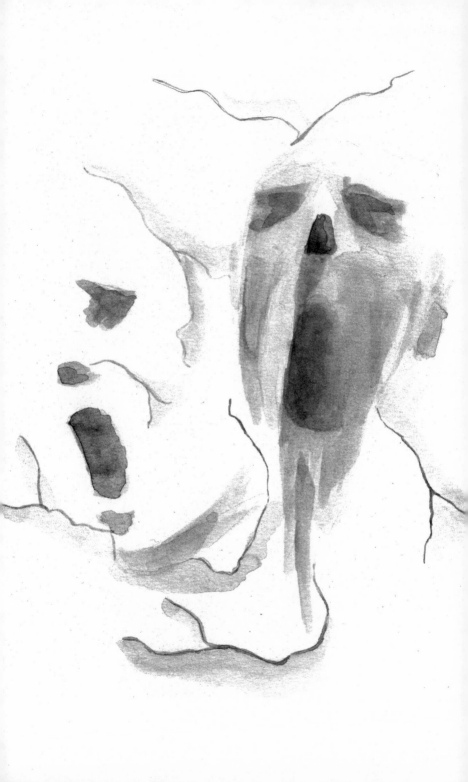

THE JOLLY JOKER
Notes and sketches by Daniele Mallarico (1940-2016),
invented for the tale *Trick*

S*eptember 5th*. At a certain point we lean over the darkness. They came into the room, they took me down to the basement. The walls were greenish, the floor foggy, the corners an earthy shade of burnt siena. I'd have liked to paint the still air, the artificial lights of the operating room, but not in that moment, not from life. I was focusing on the doctors, on the Indian nun, and I hoped they'd soon make up their minds and cut open my stomach. That way, just as quickly, they'd send me back home. The nun made me sit on the edge of the bed and stood straight before me holding my wrists. Someone bustled about behind my back. For one long minute I deeply loved that small woman, I loved her so intensely that I can't forget her. Meanwhile a prolonged wave of exhaustion settled over me and I took advantage of it, leaning my forehead between her neck and shoulder. There within that sweet gloom she helped me lie down. I saw the black bars with incredibly sharp, lengthy points that impede entry to the corner building where I live.

September 27th. It seems my body has no intention of regaining strength and I'm sick of spending time, groggy, in front of the TV. Luckily a young publisher—thirty years old at most, and so full of life that whatever he says and does offends me—asked me the day before yesterday to illustrate an edition—according to him, super deluxe—of a story by Henry James. I dallied, because the little I know about James is enough to deduce that he's a difficult writer to illustrate. But he tried to convince me, using money as leverage above all, and at least a few times with extremely self-satisfied vulgarity, exclaiming: Say yes and I'll shower you with gold. Actually when we got down to the nitty-gritty it emerged that the gold in question was practically nothing compared to what I'd gotten five or six years ago for more or less the same type of work. But what was the point of digging in my heels, niggling over a thousand euros? I don't need money nowadays, I need to feel active. Which was why we met for lunch in Corso Genova, we pretended to become friends, and we closed the deal. Starting today I've got something I enjoy mulling over. The story I have to illustrate is called "The Jolly Corner."

September 29th. I'm reading, but I get easily distracted. I was remembering the evening that my father, in a little room on the top floor of a bar in the Carmine neighborhood, lost everything he'd earned that morning in a card game. He was so tall and thin. He left the table where he'd been playing for hours, moving slowly. He put his pack of Nazionali and matches in his pocket, he said a curt, embittered goodbye to the person who'd fleeced him, and left the room. To get back down to the street he had to go down a set of wooden stairs. My father only managed a couple of steps, then he fainted and tumbled down until his face hit the ground and his front teeth cracked on the pavement.

October 4th. I realized what my father has to do with Henry James when I finished reading. Something about the text was linked to the word jolly, which is in the title, and it made me think of playing cards. Spencer Brydon, the story's protagonist, tails a ghost who is his New York alter ego. At first he does this with a certain degree of pleasure, as if it were a type of sport, a hunt, a chess match, a game halfway between hide and seek and cat and mouse. Then he gets terrifically scared and the story ends, that's it. But as I was reading I felt I recognized something, and I thought about when my father, with his whole being, even with his very breath, hoped to draw the winning cards. He was sick from playing and if, like Brydon, he'd dreamed of hunting a ghost, the ghost wouldn't have been a sullen creature like him but a cheerful, fortunate man who, by virtue of playing cards, had become a millionaire. Maybe it's because of this impression that I'm now getting interested in the joker in games where it can stand in for any card. I also looked up the history on the Internet and learned that, though it has something to do with the Fool tarot card and certain demon-like figures in China and Japan, it's really an American invention from the nineteenth century. In 1906, when James wrote "The Jolly Corner" at age sixty-three, the jolly joker, *il giocatore giulivo*, was pretty much a fledgling card.

October 10th. Am I doing too much, or not enough? Maybe too much, even though it's true that I'm struggling to get better. I live as if a part of me—maybe all of me, or at any rate the most touched-up part, the most richly detailed version—had a pressing engagement and had to leave the house as early as possible, while the other part of me—or my whole body, though reduced to a thin line, a mere outline that shadows me scarcely three feet away—reaches out a hand, weak, without tendons or veins, without even fingers, to hold me back, and says, with a barely rendered mouth: Psst, psst.

October 15th. Titles for an illustration that reproduces the facade of the house. *The Crazy Corner. The Jolly Corner. Possibility's corner.* I'm rereading the story. At first I was confused, but now I think it's a good idea to mix what James knows, and what I learn reading him, and what I more or less arbitrarily *see* isolating sentences and words. To my dismay I have to go to Betta's house, in November, but I hope to finish the work before I leave. Meanwhile I've found some images of the joker and I'd like to design a card with my father's face on it. The house in Naples harbors his ghost somewhere, along with my mother's, my grandmother's, and maybe—at least for my daughter—mine too. Investigation of shades.

October 24th. The first sign of decline is the telephone, it rings less and less. Then little by little the snail mail dwindles, along with email. I often think, good thing I'm not on Facebook or Twitter, then the signs would be even more apparent. On the other hand not using social media is itself a sign of how I ended up out of touch. Jobs, sure, they'll keep coming my way, but in dribs and drabs, not the chaotic pileup it was before. I tell myself they seek me out seldom or not at all because I'm difficult. But it's not true. The truth is that most of the people who appreciated my talents are either as old as I am, or dead, or have been pulled out of the game. It's therefore normal that my cell phone rarely rings and that I pass my days essentially shut up in the house, reading and rereading James.

I tell myself that thoroughly knowing the text is the first step to working properly. But I'm constantly distracted, what do I care about Brydon or his friend, Alice Staverton? I know perfectly well that I turn the pages, mark words or sentences, go back, reread, only to push back the moment I'll have to say: I'm done, now what?

I wake up more and more often—how should I put it— frightened. Maybe it's because of the nightly news I watch on TV before going to bed. But I've lived through times at least as awful as these and I've never opened my eyes in the morning feeling scared and not knowing why. Something inside me has deteriorated. Maybe the certainty of knowing how to react in any given situation is fading away. I have a body that's scared of its own meager reactiveness.

October 29th. James's story unnerves me. I started off full of ideas and now they all seem inadequate. Meanwhile time fades like a broken-down body. The doctor says everything's fine and that I'm lingering intentionally over my convales- cence. False. Once I used to like these psychosomatic diag- noses, now I can't stand them. The fact is I don't feel good. The doctor also said, at the beginning, that there was nothing wrong with my wife; that her symptoms were due to stress, that she'd get better if we went on a long vacation. We rented a house in the mountains for the summer, but Betta, an ado- lescent back then, complained the whole time, and Ada grew more depressed than when she was in the city. One day she said that she was going on a walk and didn't want to take her daughter, who moreover was opposed to any type of relaxing activity in our company. I sat down to work and I only real- ized that she hadn't come back when it started to pour. I looked for her in vain in the woods behind the house. I got soaked, muddy, coming back because it was dark. I saw the light on in the garage and went to see. Ada was there, read- ing, she hadn't gone for a walk. She was already an opaque woman by nature, it was tough for me to intuit her thoughts, decipher her feelings. When she got sick she turned dark, and I realized only then that she'd never told me anything truly intimate about herself. She pretended to not have an inner life.

*

October 30th. The publisher wants a few plates. Just to have a sense, he says. But I don't know what sense they'll make to him. In any case I have to start working. I'm intrigued by Spencer Brydon's chilled adolescence, which, it seems, was unfulfilling. The idea of his having an unexplored compartment in his mind might also prove useful, and a few virtues, normally rampant in his body, that have nevertheless been dormant for a while. A great deal within me also went to sleep, right at the end of adolescence. I was practically a kid, but already married to Ada, when I told a girlfriend, in an uncontrollable fit of presumption, that all I needed was a pencil to get out of anything: Naples, our friendship, marriage, love, myself, Italy, the planet.

The tinkling of a silver ring wakes me up.

November 3rd. At work. How does one draw sounds? James relies on similes. A tinkle *as of* some far-off bell. The house *in the likeness of* some great bowl, all precious concave crystal, that hums thanks to a moist finger that plays around its edge. The steel point of Brydon's stick on the marble of the pavement is easier.

November 12th. Deepest vibrations, queer vibrations. A precise, disjointed stupor. And a quiver, a flow of blood that becomes a flush. Here's where the business about the ghost is, I think. It's only thanks to the tremendous force of analogy that the vibrations, the stupor, the quiver, the flow become something *like* the unexpected occupant of

Brydon's second home in New York. The bridge that leads to the ghost, in short, is that *like*. Just let it leap and Spencer's compressed emotions produce a disquieting figure rather than a rhetorical one that roams through the huge empty house. I'd work well, maybe, if I could do the same, helping myself to a crayon, a piece of charcoal: mutating the body's flowing, quivering, stunned vibration into *something*, a presence. But I don't do a thing, I'm still bleeding, I need to get my blood count rechecked. I'll call Betta to tell her I'm not strong enough to deal with the child. She'll be upset, no doubt, but she's got to realize: She can't call and say come without thinking about anything, about my work, about the state of my health. I never asked anyone for help, not even her. And even in the event that I had asked her for it, I can safely rule out that she would have found the time to deal with me. I remember her phone call when she found out about the operation.

—Why didn't you let me know?

—It was a minor thing.

—You went alone?

—Better alone than in bad company.

—Mom would have gotten angry.

—Mom has had the privilege, for some time, of not getting angry anymore.

—What a stupid thing to say.

—It's true.

—How long were you in the hospital?

—A week.

—Everything OK?

—I've lost a little blood.

—You're crazy, Dad, you should have called me. I'll drive up to get you and bring you here.

More or less like this. She never came, of course, nor did she ever take me to her house. She made a few more calls, I'll say that, but hurried, at seven in the morning, before rushing off to work.

—How's it going, Dad?

—Fine.

—Are you still in bed?

—Yes.

—You're not getting up today?

—In a bit.

—Did you get some sleep?

—I had awful dreams.

—What did you dream?

—I don't remember.

—So why did you say they were awful?

I spoke as if I were kidding. I explained that awful dreams were a good thing at the moment, that they were useful for work. Then I added: I'm in bed but my head is full of ideas, I've been up since four.

November 18th. It sounds ridiculous, but in the end I really did try to draw vibrations, two rust-colored illustrations in which Brydon's body trembles and quivers while he gives birth, from one ear, to a little demon similar to the Joker I saw on an old American playing card. I doubt the publisher will go for it, but I don't have time to redo it, I've left for Naples. A terrible trip. In Bologna a young black guy got on, extremely well-dressed, and from that moment on all he did was holler into his phone in an unknown language. Some guy dozing across from me woke up with a start and said to him rudely, using the "*tu*": Lower your voice, why do you have to shout that way, I got up at five in the morning. The young man immediately got off the phone and started to yell at the sleepy man, this time in incredibly violent Neapolitan, full of clearly enunciated insults. The other passengers were silent, eyes lowered. I figured that they hated and feared the young brute both because he was black and because he was Neapolitan. I waited for the two of them to come to blows. I took it for granted that the moment would arrive, but it didn't. Instead there was a wearying squabble, then the white guy fell asleep and the black guy made no more calls, neither in his language nor in Neapolitan. If it had been necessary to step in, to keep them from killing each other, where would I have found the strength? And with what would I have intervened? In defense of blackness? With barely contained racism? Against rudeness, black skin or not? Using a dialect just as ferocious? I had sweats and chills for the rest of the trip, and was disgruntled upon arrival.

At Betta's house the radiators are always warm. Not at all like half a century ago. The door and windows didn't close well, the drafts were biting, in winter one died from cold. And yet I don't remember this unbearable chill, it's a new cold made in part by fatigue, in part by illness, in part by foul humor, in part from old age. This child struck me as conceited, like my son-in-law. He likes what he calls light colors. But I don't think my former illustrations of fables are dark. Poorly printed perhaps, but not dark. Saverio and Betta must have spoken ill of my paintings between them and Mario must have heard. Children gather up, with punctilious attention, words that spill from their parents' mouths.

Mario has the Joker's face.

All my life I searched for good reasons for the excessive amount of time I dedicated to my art. In the beginning I wanted to pull myself out of Naples in order to impose myself on the world. Then I thought I should represent the horrors of the world, in order to provoke the desire to revolutionize it. And finally I dedicated myself to breaking down canons, establishing new ones, experimenting, theorizing, proclaiming one thing as opposed to another. Major issues fascinated me, I feared that my smallness would have emerged without them. Ada never believed in my commitment, or maybe she only believed in the beginning. She soon thought that there was nothing capable of really involving me, that all I cared about was protecting myself, that I dodged life afraid that my organism couldn't bear it and would get hurt. Your only major issue—she once told me—is the need to turn your head the other way: *You're* not distracted, you *do whatever you can* to be distracted. She must have seen, in my distraction, what Alice Staverton, Brydon's close friend, calls *the black stranger*. I don't think it means *nigger*, no. And not someone like the young dark-skinned Neapolitan I bumped into today. But a tenebrous version of myself that had frightened her, one that sat in the dark because it was afraid of the light, a stranger who had never been welcomed, ill-mannered by nature, offensive without even knowing it. Which was why, maybe, she turned towards others she considered less black, who gave the impression that they would never grow distracted from her. Not Alice.

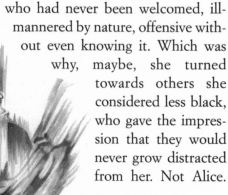

Alice holds Brydon's desolate head in her lap, welcoming everything that he is. Drawing her—I'll try it now—while she's bent over Spencer and the I, the you, the him, blur into a single awful-pleasant face that she drinks up with her eyes, without being too subtle. As far as I remember, no one had ever granted me such mercy, maybe they're things that only happen in the world of signs. You can't be truly loved.

Only now, in old age, can I agree with a concept that, in fact, I've always detested, and that is that the force of beauty is about not having motivations, not even—James writes—the ghost of a motivation. But it's too late now, the mind is what it is. I told my son-in-law, just to make small talk: I've never made a painting without searching for a major issue in order to start working. And he, politely: That makes sense, but if the paintings are small, big concepts don't render them big. He's a man who's made this way, his aggressiveness manifests itself with grace. One time—he'd come through Milan—I'd been inspired to confide in him: I think I've done everything I can do, maybe it's time to stop. Saverio immediately agreed: Yes, you're right, at a certain age you have to stop. I was upset about it, I said: Anyway, what I did counted, and I hope it will count more in the future. He answered back: Of course, you're not a Fontana, you're not a Burri, but yes. I was on the verge of replying: What do you mean, you don't know what you're talking about, what do Fontana and Burri have to do with it? But I pretended it was nothing. I'd aspired to something well beyond Burri or Fontana, even if no one would have said so, least of all Saverio. Outsized ambition dwells in undertones, ashamed of itself. But the hierarchies established by the world appear, in secret, untrustworthy. It's so avid that it can't submit to any model, any affinity, on the contrary, whatever it admires, it admires only to surpass. Sure, sure, the quintessential trousseau for truly great ambitions is failure. You only fail for greatness, not for modest goals.

The house is a huge dry shell, the rooms are empty. The vacancy, in this story, is absolute. When the *thing* that Brydon hunts shifts from mental fact to presence, to a physical image located in a physically defined space—a house on the corner between a Street and an Avenue—Spencer is terrified by it, he suspects that the other is behind a closed door that should be open instead, and just to evade confrontation, he opens a window on the fourth floor, ready to jump. The abyss, more and more often, is the way to save ourselves from ourselves.

I hated the apartment, the shape of the building, the place from which it rose, the whole city. When my parents died, I rented this house for a while, and then I left it to Betta who, after a long stay abroad, had returned to Naples. I've always loved her, but in a distracted way. All my affections were distracted affections and now it pains me a little.

The pencil has taken hold of my hand, or rather, modified it. The line, laboring as long as I'd tried to illustrate James, has turned swift, so swift that it's caused me, while I was drawing, a sort of flash-regression, I don't know what else to call it. My fingers have restored to me, at this hour of the night, the sense of being independent, the same sense I felt as a boy, when I didn't know what I was capable of and I discovered it, somewhere between amazement and fear. In brief, for a few seconds I thought I'd returned to the autonomous hand I'd had at around twelve years of age, as if my whole path as an artist—the influences that had befallen me, the way I'd inserted myself in those times trying to find my own way—had vanished. I could no longer draw the way I do now. Or I could draw, but like then.

November 19th. The shape of the ghost is the fruit of Spencer's hypothesis and Alice's dreams. A possible shape pulled forth from two clearly-defined personalities. Movement: What James doesn't narrate is the way Brydon's alter ego emerged from *indistinctness*. This, however, is what I have to do. I have to sketch the other just as he emerges from the simile and separates from Brydon, increasingly becoming a stranger to him. I'll draw some Brydons that jump out of Brydon, one totally different from another, all of them different from the real Brydon.

In the living room there's a red and blue painting of mine with a real bell in the middle of it, like those for grazing animals. The child struck it hard as if it were a door knocker and this got on my nerves. I said:

—Mario, don't do that.

—Mom lets me do it.

—Don't do it while I'm here.

—Do you want to ring it?

—No.

—Dad says if there's a bell, you should ring it.

—Not that bell. In any case, not now.

Even when I grow aware of my paltriness, I don't feel it by what I've done—decent stuff, actually, I say to myself, or at least better than that of many others—but by the levity with which I attributed to myself the ability to do what had never been done before.

I'm pausing over the climatic scene, the moment of revulsion, when, that is, the protagonist is finally able to rout out the ghost and finds it repugnant. In dialect you say *vummecà* for vomit but the petty bourgeoisie that wants to speak properly says throwing up or being sick. I feel like throwing up, I feel like being sick. There's an explicit challenge in this passage and at the same time a commonplace of representation, for example: No great artist would ever be capable of portraying in every detail et cetera et cetera. Taking out what you have in your head. Proceed by retching. Vomiting from the effort of invention. Throwing up.

The something that Spencer hunts down is a variation of his living flesh. In the beginning it dwells wrapped around his self, then it has to necessarily unfold, develop, as if it's made of a dizzying number of frames in an old-fashioned film. Here in Naples numerous *me's* were in bud since early adolescence and yearned to assert themselves, clutching at the city's thousand possible variations, because the substance of Naples is also variable, there could have been many, so many cities within it, better or downright worse than this. But they were possibilities that had brief lives, I discarded them. Or maybe I only thought I had. I wanted to try to be just one thing, nothing else, an artist

of worldly relevance, one of the few that will be remembered until the sun stops shining, or maybe even after that, on inhabitable planets, with benevolent suns. I didn't succeed, and now the old variations—defective clones, fabricated by a frustrated conscience—all rise up with unexpected force, like worms—an old simile reworked by James—when you lift a rock. Tonight, while Mario, his quarrelsome parents, the furniture, and the house all sleep, the clones appear in equilibrium, in a huge sphere, and their spellbound bodies, at present allied, lift like sinuously shaped question marks. The image could work, but I have to look for others. Variability is hard to draw. I'd like to establish the moment in which you're one way and then *you* repel yourself, just leaving the odds and ends you'll need to be something else.

What will this child become in this city? Will all his *I know*, *I'll do it*, already at the age of four, morph into a vacancy unsheathing foolish notions, inexistent skills, the sharp thirst for revenge, swagger? When did I stop telling myself I was great, considering everything I did a feat? Late, I believe. Or maybe never, not even now. I have enormous affection that grows rather than diminishes with time, for the I that I painfully chose from many, my I. How we love—all of us—our chatty little imp. The toil begins when we toss him into the world so that he's loved as much as we love him. An impossible thing. Disappointment follows the toil.

A barber's assistant, a thirteen-year-old who swept hair off customers' shoulders. Garage apprentice, turner for Alfa Romeo, workman at Bagnoli. Salesclerk and vendor of boiled pork and pigs' feet at Porta Capuana. *Camurrista* assassin, *son-of-an-oar*, slogger, trafficker, petty politician who unites the legal and the illegal, institutions to the underworld, in jail at Poggioreale. Embarking on the moneyed path: becoming a millionaire, scaring honest people, corrupting them, stealing, ravaging. Or embarking on one where the clerk complains every day at the café, reciting, between a coffee and a sfogliatella, the lines of someone who could have done more and didn't out of pride and honesty. Or standing at the window waiting for crowds of desperate people to pour out from alleys, from surrounding places, to overturn the world—who's on top goes under—and blood flows in torrents so that finally each gives according to his ability and each receives according to his need. These, and others, and still others, are the ghosts that now dart around the rooms of my adolescence. Unlike Brydon I don't need to resort to the metaphor of the unread letter, if it had been read who knows what it might have revealed. I read everything that was illegible about my existence and I know that those phantoms look like me. It would be nice if they themselves considered me a drifting shade and were terrified by the sight, but it's not the case. A long time ago, when I was twenty, I thought I'd play a part in defeating the worst citizens of Naples and, with my harsh and hopeful little works, uphold the best. It wasn't the case: The worst don't give a fuck about art, they want power, always more power, and so they keep spreading wealth and terror, thinning down the number of people who won't join them.

November 20th. I can't stand talking to the child, defining myself *Grandpa*. I'm not *Grandpa*, I'm *me*. I'm not in third person, I'm in first. But my daughter got me to talk like this straightaway, and, so as not to upset her, I started to do it. Or maybe that's not why. It seems excessive to oppose my "I" to Mario's. Better to say, even if it's saccharine: Grandpa doesn't want to, Grandpa's sorry, Grandpa will read you a fairy tale.

Brydon tends to rout out his prey with the air of the merry hunter. He's calm at the start, he takes it for granted that he'll capture something resembling him one way or the other, he has no doubt that the occupant in the house is someone like him. Instead, from one passage to the next, the mechanism of the analogy trips up. The European Brydon and the American Brydon, the refined libertine and the man who deals with real estate, have no affinity. The exception prevails upon the rule, the face of the New York ghost becomes something *indistinct* that Spencer can't fabricate anymore based on the resemblance to himself. James himself sets aside the "as" and resorts to an anomaly. One of the hands with which the ghost hides his face has severed fingers. As for Alice, I think she's in bigger trouble than Brydon. The

affectionate lady knows that two entirely incompatible projec-
tions faced each other in the house, and now the problem is
how to hold together the carefree European with the elegant
monocle and the weighted-down American with chopped fingers. The first *isn't as* the second, and yet Alice, who needs to
choose where to stand, loves Spencer and confusedly doesn't
disdain the ghost. What results is that Brydon writhes with
jealousy for a nonentity that appears to be him but in fact
isn't, but who knows, it could be. No, this doesn't strike me as
a happy ending. But seriously. One of those fibs that cause us
pain when they die is that stories really can end in bliss.

I think of Betta and Saverio. What do Spencer and Alice matter to me, I'm going to draw my son-in-law here, my daughter. Sally: this woman, too. We've exchanged a few words. She's happy to waste time chatting and I want her to think I'm nice, I have to be able to count on her to help. I've realized that she knows more than me about the tension between Betta and Saverio.

—I feel bad for little Mario, she said, far from the child's ears. People with kids shouldn't split up.

—They're not splitting up, it's just a little friction.

—You only say that because you live far away and don't hear their fights.

—It'll blow over.

—Let's hope so.

But I've realized that she doesn't hope so. On the one hand she fears that a separation would have a negative impact on this child. On the other, one intuits that she doesn't like either Betta or Saverio. It started with generic statements, such as: They're wonderful people, great professors, but they expect too much from that poor child. Then, maybe because she didn't want to badmouth Betta too much, she focused on Saverio: So much intelligence, so much attention, but then what? I agree with her.

November 21st. I woke up wanting to be punished for what I wasn't capable of doing.

In old age even the nervous system is spent, even the tear ducts.

Ada's body was a mine of information sprung from the depths of well-to-do generations and excellent education. Someone from my origins felt like he could improve just by watching, speechless, the way she moved, how she modulated her voice. She was made for others, I took her unlawfully, I forced her. Or at least this was what Betta believed ever since she was a child. She didn't realize I lived as a subaltern; her mother knew everything, I almost nothing. I was always afraid of losing her and so I defended myself by foisting the pressing needs of my presumed talent upon her. If I thought she was ignoring me I'd say:

—You don't love me.

—I love you very much.

—You love what I'm not.

—I know perfectly well what you are.

—You don't love me, then.

—You're the one who can't stand me because what's in your mind doesn't tally with me anymore.

We used to have conversations like this, we had them even after she got sick, until the day she died. I tried to wrest her from my body, from my mind. Even after reading her notebooks, I didn't stop loving her.

Mario believes he's capable of every possible feat. We had the following dialogue, more or less:

—Did you know I can pee without holding my weenie?

—No way.

—It's true, Grandpa. And the pee comes straight out, I don't do it on the floor. Can you do it?

—It's dicey.

—Not if you do it right. Try.

—Not a chance. And don't you dare, you'll wet the floor.

The child is well behaved and also out of control. He has a darting glance that surprises me. There's something physical in the expression *darting glance*: impact and speed. It's as if the eyeball—and there's nothing more blunt—takes aim and goes off to strike something in the world, violently hitting the mark. I'm sick of figurative language. I'm sick of figures, action figures, sorry figures, everything. I have to be mindful of the balcony, I'll give Saverio and Betta a good talking-to. By thinking only of themselves they haven't given a fuck about me. What ended up happening to Sally could happen to Mario, and then what would I do?

This morning I don't know if I'm scared for the child or scared of the child.